There was something refreshing and attractive about a courageous woman.

One who said how she felt and what she thought, and didn't waver on what she wanted. Or feel the need to hide the fact from others.

And just as soon as his mouth caught up to his brain and figured out how to speak again, he'd tell Sarah so.

Aaron issued himself a mental reprimand while crunching across the loose gravel in his driveway. When she'd said she hoped he'd call, his mind took it the wrong way. Clearly, she wanted to be a nanny to his boys. And clearly her statement had nothing to do with her hoping on a personal level that he'd be in touch.

Right?

At his SUV, he turned to wave to her and caught the bolts of attraction flashing back and forth between them. Okay, so maybe he hadn't imagined it. Maybe this connection did run both ways…

Books by Cheryl Wyatt

Love Inspired

A Soldier's Promise
A Soldier's Family
Ready-Made Family
A Soldier's Reunion
Soldier Daddy

CHERYL WYATT

An RN turned stay-at-home-mom and wife, Cheryl delights in the stolen moments God gives her to write action and faith-driven romance. She stays active in her church and in her laundry room. She's convinced that having been born on a naval base on Valentine's Day destined her to write military romance. A native of San Diego, California, Cheryl currently resides in beautiful, rustic Southern Illinois, but has also enjoyed living in New Mexico and Oklahoma. Cheryl loves hearing from readers. You are invited to contact her at Cheryl@CherylWyatt.com or P.O. Box 2955, Carbondale, IL 62902-2955. Visit her on the Web at www.CherylWyatt.com and sign up for her newsletter if you'd like updates on new releases, events and other fun stuff. Hang out with her in the blogosphere at www.Scrollsquirrel.blogspot.com or on the message boards at www.SteepleHill.com.

Soldier Daddy
Cheryl Wyatt

Steeple
Hill®

Published by Steeple Hill Books™

STEEPLE HILL BOOKS

Steeple Hill®

Recycling programs for this product may not exist in your area.

ISBN-13: 978-0-373-81435-0

SOLDIER DADDY

And hope does not disappoint us, because
God has poured out his love into our hearts
by the Holy Spirit, whom he has given us.

—*Romans* 5:5

I would like to dedicate this book to my newsletter "name a character contest" winners and to my many research helpers for this book. *Enormous* thanks to:

Teresa Eaves, who won the opportunity to name one of the twins. "Bryce" so well suits this little shy guy. Congrats!

Congrats to Janna Ryan who won the opportunity to help name the heroine of this book. "Sarah" totally fit!

Marcie Sheumaker, for help with all things nanny-related. Your friendship is a tremendous blessing.

Huge thanks to E. Matthew "Whiz" Buckley, Founder and CEO, The Options News Network, www.ONN.tv, who flew military combat missions for fifteen years. Thank you, "Whiz," for your outstanding service to our country. "Check6!"

Big Boo-ya! to Kelly Mortimer for connecting me with this research contact. You have a heart of gold, girl! You always fly above and beyond the call of duty.

To Patti Jo Moore (my squirrel-loving buddy!) and her nephew, Cpt. Steven B. Skipper—USAF. What an *amazing* and honorable job you have keeping our leaders safe.

To Kathy Kovack and her military family members for helping with AF lingo for every generation of servicemen. God bless your hubby and sons for serving! To Shannon McNear and Debbie Lynne Costello and their AF hubbies, Donna Moore and her AF dad, Tina E. Pinson, Carol Umberger and all other www.acfw.com members I may have missed who assisted with research. You all are the *best!*

Any remaining errors are my own.

Thanks to the Reynolds family for prompting the idea of an imaginary gaggle of geese. Only your house was stricken with an imaginary flock of unruly crows! Grin.

Chapter One

"Ooh, Aaron, she's so young! And pretty!" Mina Garcia, housekeeper and longtime family friend of U.S. Air Force Chief Master Sergeant Aaron Petrowski, clapped her dark hands together. She peeked out the Petrowski home window as the nanny applicant exited her car. The very young and vivacious applicant, very unlike the empty-nested grandmotherly types who'd interviewed so far.

Mina clutched Aaron's sleeve and continued to emit strange little squeaks as the trim-but-not-too-thin blonde crunched across a calico pattern of fallen leaves carpeting the yard he really should have raked. "Aaron Michael! Shame on you for not telling me how glaringly gorgeous she is!"

Glaringly gorgeous? That hadn't even entered his mind yesterday at the agency. What had attracted him were Sarah's on-paper credentials and her enthusiasm and gratitude over being chosen as a candidate for the job.

Trek paused, Sarah bent to pull a punctured leaf from her conservative but classy spiked heel. When she stood and eyed the house, catching a glimpse of them watching from the window, her excited wave and ready smile rivaled September's sun. Glaringly gorgeous?

Yeah, now that Mina mentioned it…

Aaron eyed Mina cautiously. "You haven't acted this excited about any of the other applicants, Mina. Please tell me you're not trying to find us something more permanent than a nanny?"

"What? Me?" Mischief twinkled from wise Hispanic eyes as she waltzed to the door with an agility and ease that told him she might have been exaggerating her "aches and pains" of late.

Though his boys could benefit from another mother, the last thing Aaron needed was another wife. The current state of his career wasn't conducive to relationships.

So why then did his heart suddenly start skipping beats as he stretched to peer around his housekeeper for a glimpse of Miss Sarah Graham, the woman he'd met at the agency yesterday?

"Hi! Hi! Come on in!" Mina grabbed Sarah's arm and pulled her inside, nearly robbing the young lady of her balance. Mina's exuberance left petite Sarah looking vaguely shell-shocked.

Mina suddenly possessed the lightness of a butterfly and the speed of a cheetah. Never before had she hugged any of the other applicants. All of them she'd eyed, hawklike, and interrogated, then shooed from his home in sputters of disgust.

Onto Mina's game, Aaron couldn't help it. He chuckled.

Sarah stepped farther inside and lifted her head at the sound. Their gazes locked for a very electric second.

A creamy glow graced her face. Layered light blond hair with trendy dark streaks fell in luxurious locks around her shoulders with every graceful movement. Wow. Beautiful indeed. Though dressed more executively today, she still looked way younger than most other applicants.

And…he should not be noticing that. At forty, he had to be at least ten years her senior. More like fifteen.

The draw of Sarah's lovely smile as she stuck out her hand to shake his made him forget what he was about to say. "Mr. Petrowski. Nice to see you again. This is Mina, I take it?" Sarah's expression went from nervous to warm when Mina vigorously shook her hand. Sarah eyed her curiously, then shifted to face him.

He cleared his throat. "Please, do come in." *Major Duh, Sergeant Goof.* She was already in. "Farther in, rather." He scratched his eyebrow and straightened his mouth to keep from laughing at himself.

Sarah started to shrug out of her jacket. She paused as her head tilted up to peer around at the jewel-toned foyer as though looking for someone. The twins, maybe?

He smiled. She'd meet the two of them in all the glory of their nearly four-year-old furor soon enough.

Mina tugged at the young woman's sleeve, helping the extraction along. "*Si,* take off this coat and stay a while."

A lo-ong while, Aaron thought, then refined his smile. He didn't need another pretty ornament around the house. He needed someone who could handle his children in their unruly moments. To safely care for them with compassion, and dare he say, love?

Aaron stuck out his hand, engulfing Sarah's in it. "Pleasure to see you again, Miss Graham…Sarah," he corrected and closed the door.

"You, too." She shifted a scuffed brown-leather backpack purse farther onto her slim shoulder. The worn item seemed out of place with her crisp, modern grayish-pink business suit and dressy heels.

His breath hitched at the stark blue of her eyes. He hadn't noticed that yesterday. "The boys are with friends until we get more acquainted, since yesterday was rushed. You can meet them another day if we move forward."

She clasped delicate hands together, but not in an obnoxious sense. "I can't wait." Sincere glee on her face proved it so.

She tucked strands of stylish hair behind her ear and peered around the large, open rooms. And at the toys his sister Ashleigh overdosed the boys with. And at the groceries and laundry strewn about.

Mina rushed forward. "You won't have to keep it clean. All he needs is someone to watch the children."

"Mina takes care of cooking and housework," Aaron agreed.

Sarah made a pleasant sound. Half laughter, half sigh of relief. "That's good to know. Though I've no trouble with housework, I'm not that great a cook. While I'm not above trying to learn, I'm afraid there would be many kitchen disasters before I mastered more than TV dinners and microwave meals."

"I'm fond of the microwave myself. Although I can grill a mean steak."

Now why had he said that? Maybe she was a vegan and he'd just offended her.

Then again, according to her dawning grin, maybe not.

"I love steak. Especially from the grill, juicy and marbled. With sea-salt baked potatoes and sweet corn on the cob dripping with hot butter. And pumpkin pie so smothered in whipped cream that you can't see the golden filling. It's my favorite meal." Because she was not much over five feet tall and he was well over six, she seemed to have to strain her neck to maintain eye contact.

He motioned to a chair in the family room. "Have a seat, Sarah."

She nodded and followed Mina into the room. The way Sarah's hands rubbed together, she was no doubt chattering out of nervousness. Her stomach growled audibly. She placed a hand against it.

He lifted his gaze from her trim middle. "Hungry?"

"I was so nervous this morning I didn't eat breakfast. And I never skip meals."

"Nervous?"

"Absolutely. This job means so much to me. I—I mean, should I end up being chosen." Rocking back, she bit her bottom lip and darted her gaze to the gleaming white marble tile.

He smiled inside. Loved that her guard slipped enough to let him glimpse some carefree as well as vulnerable parts of her.

"I'm going to my office while you two get acquainted," Aaron said to Mina and Sarah. Trying not to snicker, he retreated to his study, which also boasted a gym. Tried unsuccessfully not to feel like a total fiend for throwing Sarah to his Doberman of a housekeeper.

No nanny had passed the Mina test yet. Would Sarah?

A half-hour later, it became apparent by laughter and friendly chattering that the two were actually getting along and that there would be no bloodshed, death by spatula or shooing of the new nanny from his home today.

The new nanny. Strange that his mind would go there already. But it was true. Deep within, he felt a solid instinct that firmly stated Sarah could be it for his family.

Aaron rejoined the women. Mina rose. "I'll take care of refreshments if you'd like to show her around," she said as she passed by and breezed from the room.

Aaron approached Sarah. "Would you like to see the boys' play area and where you'd sleep if things go through?"

Her smile intensified. So did his pulse.

She rose.

"Follow me. Mina's making tea." And probably leaving them alone to get more acquainted in ways that had no business in Aaron's brain. Aaron led Sarah through the great room. He stopped at the wood banister. "You could choose any room other than, obviously, those occupied by myself and the boys."

"What about Mina?"

"She sleeps downstairs in one of the guest rooms off the kitchen. She has weak knees and trouble with stairs."

He watched her while she eyed the winding staircase. "This woodwork is absolutely gorgeous."

This girl is absolutely gorgeous.

"Feel free to look around upstairs." Aaron retreated to the kitchen and cornered Mina. "So, what do you think?"

Mina grinned like she'd won the lottery, though she never gambled. "I think you already know what I think." She winked.

Heat came to his collar for no apparent reason other than the way Mina smiled and eagle-eyed him. He fled to the formal dining room to gather paperwork that would hopefully bring his other two pararescue teams to Refuge.

Moments later, Sarah returned downstairs. "The rooms are amazing and—" Rapid movement cut her words short. Nimble feet took her to the kitchen doorway. She took the heavy, decorative wrought-iron tray from Mina, and headed to the family room.

Impressive. Pitching in already. And without her knowing, he observed her from the dining room. So her helping Mina had obviously been from pure motives and not falsity to impress him.

He made himself visible, joining them. From the tray Mina had prepared, he served the women and sat across from Sarah. "Besides being a meat-and-potatoes kinda girl who's not afraid to dive into dessert, tell me about yourself. What are you interested in and why exactly are you interested in this job?"

As Sarah spoke, her body posture relaxed.

Mina settled in a chair, forming a triangle of the three, and sipped her tea.

Every now and then he'd glimpse her mouth twitch into a privately amused grin that her dainty teacup did little to hide, as though Mina sensed his being totally enthralled by Sarah's heart and her love for children.

Yet he distinctly recalled her telling the agency owner yesterday that having children probably wasn't in her future.

While she was seemingly open and transparent in a bigger sense, he couldn't pinpoint something about Sarah. She remained a living labyrinth.

Until he determined what that something was, he'd bask in the moment and gauge Mina, whose radar would undoubtedly flip to red alert at the first sign of trouble.

Sarah's face glowed and she laughed unabashedly when Mina told of the twins' recent antics, both ornery and sweet.

"Sure you don't wanna run right back out that door?"

"Absolutely not. I never run from a challenge."

Aaron didn't doubt that.

"And the thing experts don't tell you about the terrible twos is that they last for two years." Sarah giggled.

He found himself laughing along with her. Stories rolled back and forth between the three. He couldn't recall the last time he'd had an easier, more carefree conversation.

Time to ask more questions.

Aaron rubbed his chin. "You applied to a Christian nanny agency. Tell me about your faith walk. What's your current relationship with God like?"

Aaron studied Sarah as she talked of her faith and adventures in child care. Too often he found himself smiling at the animation in her face without being sure what she'd even said. Had Mina noticed his being enraptured with Sarah? Aaron looked toward Mina's chair. Empty.

At what point had Mina gotten up and left the room?

He cleared his throat, not liking that he had been so into Sarah that he hadn't noticed Mina's departure.

"Tell me more about your education and experience caring for children." He adopted a serious tone, no longer lighthearted, and far from friendly. Like something he'd use on a Taliban defector he wasn't sure was for real.

Sarah's normally splendid smile dimmed enough to alert him she'd noticed. But soon her expressive face dazzled again as she lost herself in communicating how much she loved children. Her gestures became more exaggerated as she talked of interning at daycare centers and preschools. He loved her rendition of children's shenanigans, and found himself smiling, completely enthralled. Again.

Until he remembered why she was here.

Not to keep him company. Nor to entertain him or provide the female companionship that he hadn't known until this moment he'd been missing.

She was here for one reason only. And he wasn't the reason.

She was here to watch his precious boys. He'd do well to remember that, especially since that elusive peace he'd longed for had finally come home the very second she'd stepped inside his doorway.

Feeling a tug toward Sarah that he wasn't accustomed to or prepared to analyze, he forced his gaze to connect with his late wife's picture, the mantel centerpiece. The one memento of Donna that he kept in view, nearly four years after her passing.

And the one reminder of why he could not afford to entertain foolish thoughts of long-term with any lady.

His gaze switched to Sarah.

Not even the one who'd awakened something in him that he thought had gone to the grave with his beloved wife.

Chapter Two

How had she died?

Sarah wondered the following day as she eyed the mantelpiece photo she assumed to be of Aaron's late wife. After all, the woman in the picture held two newborn babies swaddled in blue camouflage buntings.

Adorna, the nanny agency owner, had informed Sarah that the twins' mother had died when they were eight weeks old, but she didn't elaborate. And Sarah hadn't felt it appropriate to ask.

"Welcome back." Aaron came up behind her. "Mina let you in, I see." His gaze tracked where she'd been looking: the photo. He'd entered so silently it was eerie. She gathered he'd gained the ability from being a military special operative.

Sarah forced herself to seem oblivious to the profound sadness flashing across his gaze as it brushed the image. Then in awkward silence, he lowered himself to the footstool and skimmed his solemn gaze from the glass to Sarah. His face became completely unreadable.

Understanding dawned on her. How very difficult it must be for him to have to bring a stranger in to care for her children.

It took everything in her not to rush forward and say so.

A slightly frazzled Mina shuffled into the room with a tray, breaking the moment and preventing the opportunity.

Mina looked pointedly at Aaron, still seated. "The boys are about to come unhinged. They want to know when-when-when-when-when?" She darted a head toward Sarah and raised her brows.

Sarah bit her lip to keep from giggling, because it seemed to her Mina was just as anxious as the boys.

Sarah had to admit she was anxious, too. She'd hardly been able to sleep last night due to excitement over getting to finally meet the Petrowski twins.

Aaron rose. Again, as yesterday and the day before in the nanny agency upon first meeting him, Sarah was stricken with just how intimidatingly tall and watch-tower-strong he was. Arms muscled into impressive facets made her glad he served in the job he did. If she were in need of rescue, she'd want someone this capable and strong. Blond hair with hints of starlike-silver above his ears was shaved into a military buzz. The masculine cut complemented his sturdy neck, jaw and otherwise exquisitely carved facial bones.

He gave the air a grand wave. "Let's bring in the

troops." Exiting, he went to the doorway of the playroom, said something, and came back in.

Two sets of shoes clomped across an area of tile that she couldn't see. So loud it sounded like a herd of…something. The kitchen door leading to the other end of the room banged open.

Two tiny humans who each looked like miniature Aarons in different ways bounded toward her, toting twin grins.

Her smile stretched, and her heart twisted into taffy. Twice.

Hunkered to his knee, Aaron drew them close. Tenderly, he sandwiched both in his massive arms. "Boys, I'd like you to meet someone special. This is Miss Graham. I'd like you to get to know her while I run to the DZ."

Refuge had a drop zone? Duh, of course it did. She'd been skydiving before, so she knew a DZ was a skydiving facility. Made sense. Aaron was a commander of military search-and-rescue skydiving paramedic teams, the ones who dove into danger to rescue fellow military personnel as well as dropped feet-first into disaster to rescue civilians.

She'd looked up Pararescue on her computer after the agency's owner had notified her she was a match for his family. How humbled and strikingly intrigued she'd become by Aaron after her extensive Internet and library searches. A real hero with uncommon valor and bravery.

Her attention shifted to the two beautiful boys

smiling expectantly at her. She slid to the rug in front of them. The smaller twin with the shy grin hid behind the taller one, who didn't look one bit bashful.

"Hello. You must be Braden," she said to the taller one. Tipping forward, Sarah peered at the shorter twin. "And you must be Bryce. I've heard a lot about you."

Bryce inched forward. "Do you know I like fishin'?"

"I didn't, but I'm glad I do now."

Speaking of fishing…

Five minutes with the boys and she was hooked by the gills. She shouldn't let hope rocket, but she couldn't help it. The boys had climbed into her heart as fast as they'd clomped into the room. Yes, she had a past. But she knew the person she was today. She knew with confidence she would take the best care of these precious boys.

She could only pray that Mina and Mr. Petrowski would feel the same if they discovered the epic mess she used to be.

Fortunately, he seemed the kind of Christian who maintained a close relationship with God and who led his family with faith and strength. That meant he'd hear God's voice and obey. And, hopefully, possess mercy for monumental mistakes.

Bounding forward, Braden performed a mutant wiggle dance. "And did ya know I like to play softball?"

"Really? Wow. Me, too!" Sarah tapped the brim of Braden's ball cap and smiled at Bryce. "And I also like to fish."

Truth struck Sarah like an aluminum bat to a ball.

If she didn't get this job, she'd be devastated.

Standing, she lifted her face to find Mr. Petrowski carefully watching her. She retrained her focus on the boys. An easy task, given how delightful they were.

Other than her thrice-weekly letters, her gym regimen and her child-care classes the past few years, she hadn't put her heart into anything so strenuously in a long time.

A decade, in fact.

Self-punishment, she presumed.

That she had hope for her future for the first time in a long time had to mean something, right?

If this is Your will, please give me favor with Aaron—I mean—Mr. Petrowski. Especially if those dark places of my past ever come to light.

Perplexed.

That's exactly what he felt like at the moment. What thought pattern cast dark shadows across Sarah's previously luminous eyes? Just what was the air of mystery and intrigue about her?

Mina, normally possessing unnervingly accurate radar, seemed oblivious as she went to the kitchen. Maybe he'd imagined the dismal caution in Sarah's eyes.

Aaron nodded toward the door. Sarah waved and distracted his boys while he made his escape.

"Impressive." Aaron slipped out, completely baffled at how Sarah had immediately engaged the attention of his toddlers like no one he'd ever known—

faster than foreign aircraft drew attention from air control watch towers in no-fly zones.

At the driveway, he peered in the window to study them once more. Mina stood near the family-room wall, grinning bigger than he'd seen in a while. Good to see her relaxed for once. Her blood pressure had been climbing to dangerous altitudes lately, which was another reason he needed to secure child care. Though Mina was watching them temporarily, he couldn't put the full burden on her once he returned to full-time duty.

Aaron stretched to see his boys, who stared at Sarah in wide-eyed wonder. They'd been too wrapped up in her to notice his departure.

He hoped he hadn't had the boys' enthralled, enamored look on his own face when he first saw Sarah.

She plopped back down in the floor, probably to reach eye level with his sons. Scooting close, she listened with eager, expressive eyes at something Braden was saying. Braden talked as much with his hands as with his mouth. At least Bryce wasn't having his usual Monday-morning meltdown at Aaron's leaving today. Sarah held his quiet yet rapt attention.

"Amazing."

Aaron tugged out his keys and headed for his SUV. He'd let her spend an hour with the boys and Mina. He'd have his thirty-minute meeting with Senior Master Sergeant Joel Montgomery, the leader of his local PJ team, who was also Aaron's prayer buddy, then swing back by here to observe Sarah with the boys and the boys with Sarah.

"You want the good, bad or ugly news first?" Joel asked at Refuge's drop-zone facility moments later.

Aaron pulled out his planner and pen. "Good news first."

"Thanks to our actions on Reunion Bridge after it collapsed, Refuge city council requested we take part in more community projects. They feel it will help build up town morale since our team's rapid response saved lives and made national news."

"What kind of projects are we talking?"

"For one thing, they asked us to conduct water rescue classes for local first responders. Paramedics, EMTs, firemen, police officers, Refuge River Guard, nurses, doctors, et cetera."

Aaron jotted notes while Joel talked.

"Vince Reardon offered to head that up. He also said he'd expand the program to offer it to the general public. Meaning teach laypeople, adults, children, teachers, day-care workers, et cetera, classes on basic and advanced water safety."

"And the bad news?"

"Refuge city officials want us to do more than water rescues. Our superiors are agreeable to the plan because it will help raise awareness of pararescue and help military recruitment."

"So it's a win-win situation."

"Yes, except we don't have the manpower with our

seven, eight with you, teammates. Which is the bad news. Unless our superiors agreed to station at least one more of your other two PJ teams here."

Aaron hated to break this to Joel. "No go. Least not yet. Not until I agree on paper to return to full-time, they said." And he couldn't do that until he secured child care for his boys.

Joel scrubbed his hands up his face. "May as well give you the ugly, then. Funders of the community projects have moved up their deadline by two months. Amber and I are scheduled to be out of the country then to visit the children we're adopting."

"Two months." Aaron seethed air through his teeth. "That's cutting our time in half."

Joel pulled out his calendar and pencil. "Look, if you need us to reschedule our trip overseas—"

"No. You and Amber have waited years for this."

"Tell me about it." Joel casually tossed his pencil on the pad.

Aaron picked it up and twirled it. He knew Joel felt the pressure as much as he did. No doubt they wanted to help the community. The only solution was Aaron coming back full-time. He had to do that before his superiors would station his remaining two pararescue jumper teams in Refuge and that needed to happen in order for the Refuge PJs to help the community effectively.

The way Joel sank into his chair, he looked as if he could use more good news.

"I have a nanny on the radar."

Joel's tense expression loosened. He sat up. "Seriously?"

Aaron nodded. "Yeah. If I hire her, I'll be available immediately to help get more PJs here and the community programs up and running. Name's Sarah. She's young, though."

"Single?"

Aaron nodded. "That's what her application said."

"She pretty?" Joel smirked.

"She's pretty *young*," Aaron emphasized.

But Joel's smirk didn't fade. "Oh. Right, Chief."

Silence pervaded for several seconds until Joel's amused grin morphed into an expression of thoughtfulness.

"Young might be exactly what your boys need," Joel finally said in sincere tones.

"She's certainly energetic enough. The last time Mina got on the floor with the boys like the applicant did, Mina claimed it almost took a crane to get her back up." A smile started to erupt at images of Sarah on the rug with the boys.

Joel must have noticed. He leaned in and eyed Aaron with a funny expression.

Aaron swiped all evidence of the grin from his face and cleared his throat. "So anyway, it's something to be praying about."

Joel and his own grin didn't look deterred. Best change the subject before he could probe.

"Which other projects did Refuge officials mention?" Aaron clicked his pen and poised it over his planner.

"In addition to Vince Reardon's community and military scuba diving and water safety classes, they got wind of, pun intended, Brockton Drake's wind tunnel idea. They knew we'd requested zoning for the facility in order to train military skydivers indoors during bad weather. They asked if we might also open it to the community as a family fun center and have some of our guys run it. In exchange, they offered to front half on the cost of the facility."

"Wow."

"They're also interested in Chance Garrison's rope safety training. They know he's been working with local Eagle Scouts to teach that stuff, which has been beneficial. With all the caves, bluffs and craggy hiking crevices around Refuge, local volunteer firemen and paramedics could also benefit from his training."

"Let's focus on those three programs for now. Stepping out in faith that God is drawing me back into duty, I'm going to talk to my other two PJ teams about transferring to Refuge."

"Meaning you're officially giving word and paperwork that you're returning full-time?"

Aaron nodded.

"And the nanny situation?"

"I'm confident God has it under control."

After praying with Joel, Aaron returned home. As he pulled into the driveway and exited his car, he could hear shrieks of laughter from inside. Curiosity piqued, Aaron moved faster to see. He paused at the picture window, taking in the live Norman Rockwell-ish scene in his Thomas Kinkade-like living room.

Clapping her hands, Mina tossed her head back and laughed so hard her mouth didn't close for what had to be fifteen full seconds. Aaron's gaze followed Mina's to the floor. In an undignified scramble, Sarah crawled on her hands and knees after Braden, who shrieked with laughter. Bryce scuttled from the footstool onto Sarah's back yelling, "Yee-haw! Giddy up, pony! Giddy up!"

Making very unladylike burring sounds and snorts, the previously poised Sarah moved faster, holding Bryce on her back with one hand while doing a strange-looking crawl-run-gallop thing after Braden. The entire room pulsed with fun and family togetherness, like the Rockwell and Kinkade paintings lining the guest room he couldn't bear to enter because the beautiful images of family and light felt more like a mockery in the midst of the dark sadness that had swept his home the night thieving death broke down his door and left widowhood in place of his wife.

Aaron watched through the window and swallowed. But a good kind of lump sat in this throat.

Because today was the first inkling things could be different. Aaron continued to soak in the warm scene. Sarah probably had no idea what she'd already brought into his home. Yet it was more than her. God's presence in and through her?

The sight melted something inside that had been

frigid nearly four years. All Aaron could do was stare. It seemed a miracle was unfolding before his eyes. He'd seen admirable women before but never quite like this and never quite like this *one*.

The melancholy cloud blocking his emotions for so long lifted, making way for rays of marvel to beam bright streaks through a formerly dark place as he watched. Tender sprigs of hope pushed forth.

He couldn't turn away from this atypical scene, where the sun seemed to be shining inside his house as well as outside. Nor could he remove his vision from the source of it: this glowing, vibrant woman who'd enraptured his children faster than an F-22 takes vertical flight and who had aced the Mina test with Top Gun colors.

What was the deal? He couldn't stop thinking about the Air Force blue of her eyes or the contagious sound of her laugh.

Laughter.

Something his home had been devoid of since Donna died. He couldn't change the past and he wouldn't trade his boys for anything. But his future in Pararescue and the future of quality time with his boys depended on his return to work. So did the success of community projects the Refuge city council sought for his team to bring about to heal the town after the bridge collapse. Everything rode on his ability to return to duty. Sarah seemed the key.

But things weren't always as they seemed.

He had days to decide. And his duty was divided

between his little boys and the bigger ones who understood his need to be with his children.

Overcome with emotion he hadn't felt since he'd lost his wife and plunged himself into blind survival mode for his boys, Aaron heaved a breath and watched his children with mixed emotions and mounting wonder as they danced around with this virtual stranger.

Aaron looked away, only to send his gaze searching across the sky he loved so much.

"I need Your wisdom. Outwardly she's beautiful, but You see inside a person, Father, to the very core of the heart. Only You can tell me if she's the right one to care for my sons. Help me know I'm drawn to her because of the beauty You see, and not because of what I see."

Chapter Three

"**I**'ll see who it is." Mina made her way to the trilling phone the next evening. After answering, Mina handed the cordless to Aaron. "Sarah."

Aaron brought it to his ear. "Hey, Sarah. What's up?"

"Hi. Hope I didn't wake the boys by calling."

"No, we're just getting ready for bath time."

"I'm calling to see if maybe I left my phone there. I've checked all other places I was yesterday and today and can't find it. I don't use it that often, so I didn't realize it was missing until a couple hours ago."

"Have you tried calling it?"

"Yes, but I might have left it on vibrate. I don't remember. Strange thing is, a couple of times I've called, it seemed like someone answered. Then what sounds like a small snowblower runs. Then it disconnects."

A small snowblower? Aaron eyed his boys—particularly the one with the penchant for phones and making sneak calls: Bryce. But of course there was Braden—not a day shy—who still sometimes answered the phone at times when Aaron's voice came across the answering machine before Mina could make it to the cordless. Small snowblower did quite accurately describe Braden breathing into a phone before he spoke into it.

Aaron tuned back into Sarah.

"…then it goes to voice mail. I'm afraid the battery will die soon and I won't be able to find it."

Aaron rose and looked around the sitting room where Sarah had romped with the boys. "I don't see it at first glance, but I'll take a better look and call you back."

"Thanks, I appreciate that."

Aaron hung up and moved the footstool. No phone.

Bryce approached cautiously, finger in mouth. "Whatcha doin' Daddy? Who was on the phone?"

On his knees, Aaron angled toward Bryce. "Miss Sarah. I'm looking for her phone. She might have lost it here. Have you seen it?"

Bryce's eyes grew wide. He faced Braden, who suddenly avoided Aaron and streaked past the bathroom.

"Son?"

"Um…" Bryce looked ready to flee or cry. He darted guilty looks toward the stairs, where Braden now half slunk, half tiptoed upward.

And suddenly Aaron knew. One of them had the phone.

He could go ahead and call it, hoping to hear it

vibrate or chime, but he wanted to give the mini-criminal a chance to come clean first.

"Bryce? Do you know where the phone is?"

He gnawed his finger. "Um. Maybe."

"Does Braden have the phone?"

Bryce shook his head with vigor. "He doesn't have it."

"Does he know where it is?"

"Maybe."

"Do you?"

"No. Please don't be mad at him, Daddy."

Aaron rose. "Braden? Come down here, please."

Braden had never descended stairs so slowly. "What, Dad?"

"Do you know where Miss Sarah's phone is?"

Braden fidgeted so much the banister jiggled.

"Son?" Aaron lengthened the word and firmed his tone.

"I don't have it!"

Aaron drew a breath, hoping to inhale patience along with oxygen.

God, help Braden want to be honest. And help me deal with this right so he learns integrity.

Aaron picked up his cell phone and typed in Sarah's number. Seconds later a musical tune sounded from the playroom.

Bryce gasped. Braden's eyes bugged.

"Busted."

He must not have heard the chime before due to the solid-wood door being closed.

Aaron tilted his chin at Braden, frozen to the stairs. "Go get it. Now." Aaron's tone left no room to refute or resist.

He dialed Sarah back at the number in the caller ID and let her know the phone was there. "I'll call you right back, Sarah."

Braden shuffled like an endangered snail to the other room. His ploy when he didn't want to do something or when he was in trouble was to feign fatigue.

"Get a move on. Or get used to no cartoons."

Braden sped up considerably, then returned with the phone outstretched. "I didn't mean to steal it." Braden's chin wobbled. At least he looked contrite now.

Aaron sat and pulled Braden onto his lap. "Then why did you take it, son?"

"I just borrowed it so she would come back and get it."

Bryce moved close. "Yeah. We like Miss Sarah and want her to come back."

Aaron nibbled his bottom lip. At least Braden hadn't lifted the phone solely for the sake of stealing it. "Taking her phone wasn't the best way to go about making her want to come back though. Was it?"

The boys shook their heads.

Aaron called Sarah's landline again. "I'll bring your phone by so you don't have to use the gas. But first, I have a couple of boys who'd like to say something."

"Okay." Sarah sounded mildly curious.

He passed the phone to Braden.

* * *

As Sarah sat at the tiny motel-room table preparing to write one of her thrice-weekly letters, whimpers came across the line, causing her to pause.

"Mi-iss Sarah?"

Bryce or Braden? She couldn't be sure. "Yes?"

"I—I—I— Please don't be mad at me and not come back."

Sarah's heart melted. "Is this Braden?"

"Ye-heaw."

"Do you have something to tell me?"

Sniffles. "Uh-huh."

Shuffling came across the line. Then in the background she heard Aaron's voice, softly coaching Braden. Then what sounded like an escalating,"I-don't-want-to-I-don't-want-to-I-don't-want-to," then a minor scuffle then sniffling back on the line.

"M-Miss Sarah, I took your phone."

"Oh. Why? Did you just want to play with it?"

"No-oo. I wanted to play with you."

Sarah covered the phone and turned her mouth away. Easier to quell the laugh. "You thought if you took my phone that I'd have to come back. Is that it?"

"Uh-huh."

"Yes, ma'am," Aaron whispered in the background.

"Yes, ma'am," Braden corrected in a wobbly voice.

"Well, how about if I want to come back on my own? Wouldn't that be better?"

"Uh-huh. Daddy says, wait…" The sound of a hand muting the phone but not covering it completely.

"What did you say, Daddy?" Then Braden's windlike breath came back across the phone. "He says it's not wrong to wanna see you again. Just how I took the phone to get my way wasn't right."

A deep male voice from the background: "And I'm sorry."

"And I'm…wait. Daddy, why are *you* sorry?"

A sigh. Then an Aaron-size chuckle. "Not me, son. You."

"Oh. I'm sorry, Miss Sarah."

"I forgive you, Braden. And I hope we get to see each other again, too. Your daddy loves you and your brother very much. So much that he wants to be very sure to pick the right nanny. If that's not me, then God will send someone better. Do you believe that?"

"Guess so."

"So you learned a lesson today. Sometimes I've learned lessons the hard way, too."

"You did?"

"Yup. But you're a good boy and I know your daddy knows that."

"'Kay. Bye." More shuffling.

Then, "Sarah?" The deep baritone of the father whose voice should *not* make her want to swoon or melt. But did nonetheless.

"I'm here." *But wish I was there.*

"Thanks for being so gracious with forgiveness."

Please return the favor. "No problem."

But there was a problem. Braden's innocent words rang in her head like a gong.

Daddy says it's not wrong to want to see you again.

Why did her mind question whether it was wrong to hope the boys' father wanted to see her again, too?

"If you'll shoot me your address, I'll run this phone by."

Nor could she deny the hope lifting her joy and her pulse in anticipation of seeing Aaron again.

Sarah fumbled with reciting the address. "If you want to bring the boys, that's fine."

"They'd love to come see you, but bedtime looms."

"Ahh, yes. Very important to keep schedules consistent."

"Especially since their emotional equilibrium is a little off with me returning to work."

"Would it be better for me to come there to get my phone?"

"No, then the boys would be too riled to sleep. Besides, that'd reward Braden for taking your phone and Bryce for hiding the fact from me. Especially since they did so to force you back. I'll just bring it by."

"Okay." Sarah hated for Mina to have to do the bedtime ritual alone. "If you need to wait until the boys are bathed and settled to come over, that's fine."

"That'd be good. I'll help Mina put the boys down to sleep first if you don't mind waiting."

"I don't have anywhere to be."

"Great, then. See you in a bit."

The call disconnected, but she could still imagine his voice on the line. *See you in a bit.* She melted at the notion.

Then she remembered she was wearing her oldest pair of snarled-leg jeans with her favorite—but falling apart—flip-flops.

She surged to her closet and searched for something nicer. She flipped through hangers, struggling to convince herself she was trying to impress Aaron her potential boss and not Aaron the drop-dead gorgeous man.

Sarah shoved down flares of attraction trying to ignite in her mind. Fended off fond remembrances of the way he said her name, of how deep and rich and soothing-suave his voice was. How intent and coordinated he looked when he walked: sure and solid yet graceful and sublime.

"That's it." She'd nip this nonsense right now. Sarah reached blindly and yanked a shirt, any shirt, from a hanger, vowing she'd wear whatever her hand landed on. The material slid off into her fingers, which recoiled at the feel of steely, pokey wool.

The closet mocked her like an open, laughing mouth.

Great. The ugly unisex fruitcake cardigan her family passed around at Christmas. Year after year they'd rewrap it and send it to someone else. Sarah had managed to avoid it until this year. It was four sizes too big, but oh, well. She must endure her choice and ensure her motives were pure.

After throwing the cardigan over her pink, paint-splotched T-shirt, Sarah intentionally resisted the urge to rush to the bathroom and freshen up her hair and makeup before he came.

She stood in front of the motel dresser mirror and

pointed a finger at her reflection. "Don't feed this attraction. Don't. And it will starve into nothing."

Deep inside, she knew she wanted this for the boys.

She sat on the creaky bed and picked up her Bible. *"Please order this attraction back in its place,"* she asked God and opened to where she'd started reading this morning.

Then she sat to write her letter.

I pray you always have people in your life who love and care about you. I wish you a full life. I'm sorry I might have taken that away. I pray for you every day. Not a day goes by that I don't think about you and wonder how you are. I'm sorry for my choice beyond what words can say. With love, Sarah.

She stamped a flower on the front of the envelope and fancied it with her embosser. Sunflower this time. She rose and eyed the sparse parking lot. The clock. Paced the small room. Pondered how heavy a responsibility it would be to find the most well-suited long-term caregiver for those little cuties, who were obviously Aaron's cherished treasures.

"And please, for their sake, let me have this job. I know I'm right for it. For them. Help Mr. Petrowski know that, too."

"Could this be it?" Aaron stepped from his SUV into the parking lot of a run-down motel in the bad part of town. The sort of shady that had nothing to do with trees.

One of the unit doors opened. Sarah, dressed in a gaudy top and worn jeans, stepped out. "Hi there."

"Hi." He held out the phone and tried not to balk at the horrific attire. "Here's the evidence."

She laughed and stepped forward, reaching. Their hands brushed with the transference of the cell.

He paused, endeared at how her cheeks matched the color of her pink shirt beneath the V-neck of her old, Army tent-looking sweater. One that looked as if it had waged a war and lost. Still experiencing a zing in his fingers, he shoved his hands in his pockets at the same time as she fumbled her phone into hers.

"So," they said simultaneously, then laughed.

"You live in a motel?" Aaron rocked back on his heels to view the buzzing sign, missing the first and last letters. "Or should I say an 'ote'?"

Her shy smile faded. But only for a second. "For now. It's a lot nicer inside than the outside looks."

He peered around the neglected neighborhood. Same area where Celia Munez, now Peña, wife of team member Manny, lost her first husband. He was killed here during a drug bust years prior to her meeting Manny. The team had talked of ways to reach out to the area's gang-prone teens and their families.

"This isn't exactly the safest part of town."

"I figured that out. I plan to get a better place. I just wanted to wait until…"

Her voice trailed but he knew her thoughts. She

wanted to wait to see if she got this position as his boys' nanny, for if she did, she'd have a place to live. But until he was one hundred percent certain she was it, he couldn't give her false hope. Still, he hated for a young woman like her to be living in a place like this.

"I'm sure you'll find something better soon." He offered a reassuring smile.

She studied his face, then nodded. Yet her uncertain expression suggested she held doubt over getting the job.

Throat cleared, he hesitated a moment, deciding how best to word this. "I'm not that good at telling people how I feel. I'm better at giving orders and controlling insubordination." He cleared his throat again. "But I just wanted to say thanks."

"For?"

"Yesterday. I've never seen my children laugh that hard for that long. Ever."

She looked momentarily disturbed. Same way he felt.

"Whatever you brought to our home that day, Sarah, don't ever lose that in your life. No matter how things work out with us, I mean, with this job."

She nodded. He was surprised to see moisture sheen her eyes. He stuffed his hands deeper in his pockets to keep from tending to the lone tear streaking down her face. The back of her hand swiped it away like a pesky mosquito. Fidgety, she gathered gobs of that overgrown eyesore of a sweater and twisted its hem in her small hands. Her frazzled mood matched the sweater. She didn't seem the type to cry. So why did she?

He shifted his feet, which ached to go to her. "What did I say that upset you?"

Her shoulders rose then drooped. "It just seemed the kind of speech a person gets before they get let go, is all."

Did she not know? Letting her go was the last thing on his mind right now. Seeing her luminous eyes and lips swollen with emotion and the way moonlight played with hair as shiny as gold…

He swallowed. "I have no reason to think you won't get the job. But I also live under the logic that if something seems too good to be true, it probably is."

She gave an unexpected laugh. "In other words, you're looking for my fatal flaw?"

"Guess so. I like your bluntness, by the way."

"I prefer to think of it as transparency." Her smile faded and her eyes dimmed. "I am flawed, Aaron. But I've learned and grown from the mistakes of my youth. Some really big mistakes."

"We all have." He shifted. "And you're still young."

"Which means I'll make more mistakes?"

"No, I meant that… I guess I'm not sure what I meant."

"If you choose to trust me, you won't be sorry. But if this isn't meant to be, then there's someone better for your family. Trust your judgment."

He nodded, amazed at the level of wisdom riding her young words and the power of conviction driving them. Whether she ended up being their nanny or not, this was an extraordinary woman. One he'd not soon forget if things didn't work out.

"Now, get back to those beautiful boys and watch them sleep. Give Mina my regards." She stepped back toward the concrete landing that ran flush with the drab units.

At the sudden proximal distance, Aaron experienced a dip of disappointment. Surprised himself with acknowledgment that once here, he didn't want to leave her presence.

The way she paused and tapped her toe on rotting boards meant to be someone's lame attempt at landscaping, maybe she felt the same.

September's late evening breeze lifted silken hair off slender shoulders and swirled fallen multicolored leaves behind her. Stepping away from the wood and onto the gravel lot toward him again, she rubbed her arms. "Chilly for fall."

"I think we're expecting a harsh winter. I should let you get inside out of the cold. Again, sorry about the phone."

"No need to apologize. I understand."

He backed up a step and tried to think of something intelligent to say to exit the conversation, but his brain felt first-date awkward. Weird. "So, I'll be in touch."

"I hope so."

Aaron turned to go with her softly spoken words streaming across his heart, slipping past barriers he'd spent years steel-bolting against such feminine wiles. Yet he was certain she had no idea the effect she stirred in him. How her voice melted the metal off the chains around his heart. Guileless. Words issued one breath beyond a whisper. Yet her honesty gushed. And it echoed his thoughts right now.

I hope so, too.

At the concrete bumper near the gravel lot, he paused to look over his shoulder.

And found her, arms crossed over her belly, watching him. Half hunched over, almost as though in pain.

Yet she smiled. Or tried to, with a dreamy expression she seemed pained to carry.

Why on earth would it hurt someone to dream? To hope?

He knew why.

Because dreams could die when dashed and shattered hope could slice like shards of broken glass.

And suddenly he recognized the look in her eyes.

Because he'd seen it in the mirror every day for years.

The look of a tempest-tossed person who'd been sloshed overboard by life's most wretched waves and nearly taken out.

He knew his.

What had been her storm?

And why was he standing here staring as if desperate to draw it out of her? He became fully cognizant of how Sarah shifted beneath his gaze, as if she was growing uncomfortable under the weight of it.

Yet she didn't look away either.

What on earth was this sea-size magnetic pull?

And would it fade? Remain the same? Or grow strong enough to weather life's storms?

As if sensing the draw, too, Sarah shifted and

stepped back—almost stumbled—until sharp edges of moonlight carved her face into shadows.

With a slightly awkward wave, she turned. Jogged up the steps.

But he remained.

She all but melted into the safety of her open door, yet didn't close it. Nervous fingers tugging at frayed ends of the multicolored hobo sweater's sleeves, she faced him again.

He nodded at her and turned to go. And was immediately accosted by a revelation that suggested an old war-torn Army tent never looked so good. Thoughts and images assaulted his every step. Even that bulky, unattractive sweater hadn't been able to hide her physical beauty, which he felt guilty to find so appealing.

There was something refreshing and attractive about a courageous woman. One who said how she felt and what she thought and didn't waver on what she wanted. Or feel the need to hide the fact from others.

And just as soon as his mouth caught up to his brain and figured out how to execute speech again, he'd tell Sarah so.

And another thing…Aaron issued himself mental reprimands while crunching across loose gravel. When she'd said she hoped so, his mind took it the wrong way. Clearly, she wanted to be a nanny to his boys. And clearly her statement had nothing to do with her hoping on a personal level that he'd be in touch.

Right?

At his SUV, he turned to wave, and caught the bolts of attraction flashing back and forth between them. Okay, so maybe he hadn't imagined it. Maybe this fizzing connection did run both ways.

Which could be detrimental to them all. Especially his boys, should they get attached and Sarah bail if something went awry. Aaron eyed the neighborhood, then intently held her gaze.

"It isn't safe, Sarah. Please lock your doors."

And those of your heart.

Better for us both that way.

Chapter Four

"I can't imagine what happened. I never leave it unlocked," Sarah said of her car to Adorna in the nanny agency's lobby the following week.

"Was anything taken?" Adorna asked, entering her office and flipping on the light.

Sarah followed and took her usual seat across from the agency owner. "All my CDs. But they're mostly modern worship, Christian rock or songs with a positive message. So maybe the person who broke into my car and took them will have a change of heart."

"We can hope."

"We can also change the subject." Sarah forced a laugh and stuffed the police report into her purse. "Aaron was right about the bad neighborhood." What would he think if he knew she'd been robbed after he'd warned her?

"Speaking of, what did you think?" Adorna folded her hands.

"The boys are absolutely adorable."

Adorna's brows arched. "And Mr. Petrowski?"

Heat rushed her face when she remembered their last encounter, when he'd dropped off her phone, and the complete weirdness surrounding his departure. Surely it had been the full moon. And nothing more.

"Wasn't nearly as scary as I feared," Sarah hedged.

Adorna adjusted her glasses while she opened a manila file. "Then I have good news for you. Mr. Petrowski has requested another session with you."

Sarah stifled a squeal. After all, she wanted to maintain some semblance of professionalism. "Awesome!"

"In addition to him conducting a more in-depth interview, you'll need to prepare a list of questions to ask as well. With this moving into the next phase, there's really only one final step before decision time. Did you read his contract?"

Sarah nodded. "Yes. I'm okay with everything in it."

"Mr. Petrowski has requested that you spend time with the boys several days this week, starting tomorrow."

"Sounds great. I'm really excited to see the boys again."

And the dad.

Stop! She scolded herself. She needed to be all about the job and not about the man whose intense eyes and smile and radio-quality voice could snatch away a woman's breath.

"I think you'll be the best thing that's happened to this family in a long time, Sarah."

"Thank you for believing in me."

"Of course. And so you know I mean that, I'm waiving fifty percent of the placement fee when Mr. Petrowski signs you on as his sons' nanny."

Sarah laughed. "Don't you mean 'if'?"

Adorna shook her head. "Unless something drastic goes wrong, or you're not what he thinks, I'm ninety-nine percent sure you have this job."

…not what he thinks…

Again, Sarah's past tried to pull out in front of oncoming hope to slam her head-on with old guilt, shame and unworthiness.

What I did is not who I am anymore.

Growing up, she'd dreamed of having her own family someday. God would probably try to work that deflected dream back into her deflated heart. But for now, more than anything, she wanted to be there for *this* family.

Unless you're not what he thinks.

Aaron didn't know about her past yet. What about when he discovered it? But she wasn't that person anymore.

Right?

Then why did cold hands of guilt press sharp fingernails into the shoulders of her resolve as she walked out of the nanny placement agency?

Was she still punishing and not completely forgiving herself?

Or was this feeling God niggling her to tell Aaron about her past before he made his decision? And if so, when?

Help me know.

* * *

"Did you know Mina speaks spinach?" Bryce said to Sarah, moments after she arrived for her next visit.

"Sp—" Laughter sputtered past the rest of Sarah's word. "Spinach?"

"Yeah. Haven't you ever heard of it?" Bryce blinked.

"Not quite that way," Sarah said, figuring Bryce meant "Spanish" instead.

Aaron pressed his chin into his knuckles and studied her, as if to discern how she had drawn out the more withdrawn of the two boys. "Bryce has a language all his own. Hardly ever talks, much less to strangers.

"Braden is more outgoing. Definitely the extrovert. He's usually the first to get in trouble," Aaron whispered.

"And Bryce is usually first to let us know about it." Mina waved a kitchen towel as she laughed.

"So, Bryce is the informant," concluded Sarah.

Aaron grinned. "And Braden is the enforcer."

The adults shared a laugh as the boys played across the room. Bryce picked up a plastic motorcycle and inched toward Sarah, then changed gears and stuffed himself under Aaron's arm.

"Bryce is my shy boy." Aaron pulled the child onto his lap. "And that's okay, huh, buddy?"

Bryce leaned into Aaron and peeked at her between his fingers. He flashed a beautiful, bashful grin.

It heartened her that a strong military man like Aaron was okay to let his gentler, more sensitive son be himself.

Sarah leaned forward. "So, boys, besides fishing and softball, tell me what you like to do."

"Lotsa stuff." Making revving sounds, Braden ran the motorcycle across the air in front of Sarah.

"That's a nifty bike." She brushed a finger along his toy then Bryce's. "I've never seen others like them."

"Uncle Vinny gave 'em to us," Braden said.

"Vince Reardon is on one of my military teams. Although he tends to want people to think he's hard-nosed, tough and brooding, he's crazy about kids and bikes. He had his sister weld those for the boys." Aaron intercepted the bike as it swerved near a lamp. It amazed Sarah how lightning-fast his hand struck. What was he saying?

"He's not really their uncle but they call him that."

"Interesting."

"Excited to spend more time with them?"

"Yes!" Sarah pulled out her backpack. "I brought coloring books, crayons and cars."

The boys abandoned the cycles and swooped in on her.

"I want the cars!" Braden zoomed his hand up and jumped.

Bryce eyed the coloring book with reserved interest.

She tugged out some pages and a pack of crayons. "Something tells me you like to draw." She eyed faded ink marks on Bryce's arms and legs, which someone had obviously tried to scrub off but couldn't completely.

Bryce took the pages.

Aaron leaned his chin toward them. "Boys, what do you say?"

"Thank you, Miss Sarah," Bryce said in a small voice. Then he grinned. Her heart melted. He had his daddy's slight dimples. She hadn't noticed that before, since Bryce didn't often smile.

"Yeah. Thanks very much!" Braden shimmied and bounced in berserk motions, like a barely coiled ball of energy.

Aaron slid Bryce off his lap. "Okay, boys. Hugs. Daddy has a meeting."

Panic entered Bryce's eyes. "Can we go?"

"Not this time, buddy. You get to spend time with Miss Sarah. Okay?"

His lips trembled. "Okay."

Aaron hugged Braden, then Bryce, who clung to his father's neck. Panic mounted on Bryce's face and he broke down. Aaron looked torn. Pangs of compassion squeezed Sarah for them both.

Bryce clung to Aaron's neck. "Daddy, don't go!"

Poor thing. He was having a hard time with his dad returning to work. And getting to know her, a virtual stranger.

Aaron knelt and gave Bryce another hug. "I know, buddy. It's hard for me, too." He closed his eyes and swallowed, offering Sarah a glimpse of a surprisingly vulnerable side. Yet it only served to strengthen his image in her eyes.

How would he extract himself from Bryce's crawfish grip? She could help. Use distraction.

She stood so she was at eye level with Bryce. "Hey, Bryce, can I tell you a secret?"

As Aaron tugged the boa constrictor that was Bryce from around his neck, Sarah held out her arms. Bryce inched toward her with the tip of his finger in his mouth. Tears glistened in eyes that struggled to trust and to understand.

Pulling Bryce close so Aaron could make his escape, Sarah cupped her hand around Bryce's ear. "Want to help me make a project for your daddy while he's at work?" she whispered.

An instant smile lit his face. She could imagine any brighter would have caused the room lights to flicker. The kid's grin pulled a lot of juice. She hoped to see it more often. She'd prayed for God to help the boys adjust and cope with Aaron leaving for work. *Thank You for answering.*

"Yes," he said. His dimples reemerged.

"It'll be fun. I promise."

"What?" Braden approached.

"Come here," Sarah said.

"I want to tell him!" Bryce leaned toward Braden and whispered.

Braden jumped up and down. "I know a surprise! I know a surprise!"

"Shh." Sarah held a finger to her mouth and gave Braden and Bryce exaggerated winks. "It's a secret plan."

Mina reentered. After a brief exchange of conversation with Aaron that he initiated in tones Sarah couldn't hear, Aaron stepped toward the foyer. "See you later, boys. Ladies." He tipped his head at them and cast Sarah an expression of gratitude. The door closed behind him.

With a quick smile, Mina eyed her watch, slipped from the room and disappeared somewhere.

Sarah settled near the boys. "I'm so excited we get to make a project for your dad while he's gone." The more craft items she pulled from her backpack, the wider the boys' eyes grew. Glitter glue. Bendable pipe cleaners in every color. Scissors with differently shaped blades. Foam shapes. Washable markers and stencils.

"This is gonna be fun!" Braden exclaimed.

"Yeah," Bryce added with more exuberance than she'd seen before.

Good. Seemed she was winning over the hearts of the little guys. Her eyes veered toward the window, where Aaron's truck left the long, barren driveway.

What about the big guy?

What a way to win hearts. Coloring pages and crayons. A nanny's staple.

Now he knew what she kept in that bulky backpack. She'd brought projects and toys for the boys.

"Smooth move, lady. I like you already," he said appreciatively and eyed his house through his SUV's rearview mirror.

Aaron had fed the boys an extra healthy meal and, as usual, had foregone any sweets this morning. So they wouldn't be grumpy from low blood sugar today with Sarah.

Remembering Bryce's tears tugged and tore at his heart. But Sarah had come to his rescue. Without her help, Aaron had no idea how he would have gone on to work. Unintentional or not, kids knew how to slather on the guilt.

Ten minutes later he pulled into the parking lot of the Refuge drop zone. Joel's Expedition already sat in the lot beside the rest of the team's vehicles. Aaron must be the last to show.

Once inside the massive brick-fronted pole barn structure, Aaron pulled Joel and Manny Peña aside. "Hey, be in prayer about this. I know there is a lot riding on whether I can come back to active duty now or not. I found a nanny who I think will work out so I can."

"Same one you mentioned before?" Joel asked.

Aaron nodded and motioned over the rest of the seven-man team, mostly to avoid Joel's overly curious undertones.

Scrapes sounded as Manny turned a chair around and sat, straddling it. "So, we going forward with the plans Refuge city hall asked us to participate in to try to boost the town's morale? It really took a nosedive when the bridge collapsed."

"Yes." Aaron said. "We'll move forward in the planning stages of the water and rope safety classes as well as the wind tunnel idea."

"But, in order to do that, you need to bring more PJs

to the area, right?" And in order to do that, he had to return to duty full-time.

Aaron nodded. "The nanny is with the boys now. She's agreeable to signing on for an extended time."

Manny shifted in his chair. "You sound hesitant, Aaron. We understand that you need to put your boys first."

Aaron shook his head. "It's not that I don't think she's safe or anything. It's just that she's drastically younger than other nannies who've applied." He felt himself blush. By the looks of the team's sharpening gazes as they crowded around, they noticed, too. Aaron wasn't trying to be sexist and he hoped his hesitation with offering her the job didn't seem discriminatory. "Truthfully my mind may just be scrambling for excuses because I feel guilty returning to work."

Not only was he uncomfortably taken aback by her zest and beauty… "My main concern is she'll want to start a family of her own sooner than she thinks. Then I'd be out of a live-in nanny. And the boys would have to get used to another stranger coming in and caring for them when it should be—"

Their mom. Aaron clamped shut his mouth but the respect and compassion streaming from the eyes of his men let him know their minds also finished out his thought. None of the men had blamed him when he'd pulled out of the dangers of Pararescue to care for his infant twins when their mother had died.

"Anyway, she's willing to sign a legal document

stating she won't have another commitment during our contract that will interfere with her priority."

"So it's all good, right?" Manny asked.

"You'd think." You'd also think that if he was looking for someone with no other commitments he'd want someone younger, as they'd be less likely to be attached to their own family. "But it perplexes and saddens me that a young, beautiful single woman doesn't feel she has a future in sight as far as her own family." Adorna, the agency owner, had mentioned that to Aaron; Sarah had alluded to it in conversation as well.

"Young?" Chance's head whipped around.

"Beautiful?" Brock sat straighter.

Vince stepped closer. "Single?"

"So," Brock said, "when can we meet her?"

Aaron pumped the air with his palms. "Whoa. Down, boys. She's a respectable girl. A devoted Christian. Not your type."

"What about your type, Petrowski?" Vince folded massive arms across his black T-shirt-covered chest. And smirked.

Aaron shook his head. "As I said, she's young."

"You're not exactly a dinosaur, Chief," Chance said.

Manny waved a vague hand in the air. "Yeah, age is a matter of the mind. Long as you don't mind, it doesn't matter."

"Long as she's legal," Vince said. "She legal?"

Aaron shot him a withering look. "She's legal. And off-limits. To all of us. Especially you. End of story."

"So, back to the business at hand." Joel rested his forearms on the tabletop.

Pivoting, Aaron faced the rest of the guys. "Here's the plan. I'll contact the other PJs I command. See who's willing to transfer to Refuge Air Base. That way we're not putting the community programs totally on a back burner when conducting regular pararescue trainings and in the event of being away on missions. Once I get all three teams here, we'll rotate so that one team will always be in Refuge to man the community projects while another team is on training ops, which leaves the third team for emergency missions. My other two teams haven't been together as long as you guys. Regardless, my bet is they'll jump at the chance to have a stationary base of operations. You guys are somewhat of an icon to them. Most of them are fresh, just out of Pararescue and don't yet have families."

"So no baggage?" Vince said.

Manny jabbed his arm. "Hey. Watch it. I don't consider my family baggage."

Joel straightened. "Me neither. And you'd better hope Celia doesn't get wind of you calling her a bag." His mouth twitched.

"Yeah, she'll slug you, then laugh about it," Nolan said.

Ben snickered.

Aaron eyed his watch and cleared his throat.

The room straightened up and misconduct ceased.

Aaron grinned inside. He still had it.

Though he hadn't been in the picture much the past

few years, they still respected his authority. The teasing and razzing could be relentless, but these guys wore respect for their superiors as proudly as their crisp maroon berets.

Hard-core honor, uncommon valor and selfless bravery defined every one of them. They'd throw themselves in front of a bullet if it raced toward their teammates or their leaders. Aaron knew that was mostly because the guys knew he and Joel would do the same for them.

Aaron pressed his hands on the table. "I'll contact non-Refuge team members one or a few at a time, have them check out the facility and observe the programs we're instituting. Decide if they want to transfer. Until then, move forward with objectives we mapped out in the last meeting with city officials."

"So in short, proceed as planned?" Joel asked.

"Yes." Aaron eyed his watch. "I have another errand to run. We still on for Saturday evening at your place, Joel?"

"Need you ask?" Chance grinned. "Dude always has us over on weekends."

Joel rose. "Yep. Same time. Same place. Cookout, my house. Six o'clock."

"What about when you and Amber go overseas?" Nolan asked. "We'd feel weird meeting and greeting at your place without you there."

"Not to mention Joel's having renovations done to add bedrooms for all the kids they want to adopt," Manny said.

Joel rose. "I'm sure you guys will find an alternate place to meet while we're gone. Until then, we're on for every weekend like usual. As always, everyone bring a side dish and a two-liter of soda. We'll take care of the meat."

"Okay. See you at six on Saturday," Aaron said, wishing he hadn't let his yard go. If he got it cleaned up, he could have the guys over. Plenty of space and stuff for kids to do.

The group started dispersing.

"Yo, Petrowski. You should invite the new nanny." Brock smirked all the way to the counter, where Vince grabbed his motorcycle helmet.

"She's not the new nanny yet, Brock." He turned to go. "But if I do decide to get a wild hair and invite her, mouths shut. Eyes and minds off. Do I make myself clear?"

"What about hands?" Vince asked in baiting undertones.

"You so much as think about touching her, even accidentally, you'll lose flesh courtesy of my favorite lethal weapon, Reardon. You hear?"

"Yeah. Loud and fifty-caliber clear." Uncharacteristic humor resided in the tall PJ's normally brooding eyes.

Brock grinned. "We get it. You just want her for yourself."

Aaron laughed because a smile danced in Brock's eyes when he said it. But as Brock's declaration rang in his head, heat flashed under his skydiving jumpsuit collar.

Teasing subdued, the guys triggered fully-loaded looks at one another in semiautomatic sequence.

Aaron didn't have to wonder why.

They'd all tried to set him up numerous times in the past several months. Manny's fiery, outspoken wife, Celia, known for aggressive matchmaking, had gone as far as telling him Donna wasn't coming out of the casket so he should get his heart off its broken duff and date.

But he'd always adamantly repelled their attempts at steering him toward another romance.

He didn't want to ponder why he didn't feel so inclined to strenuously resist, evade or negate their efforts this time.

Chapter Five

After overseeing PJ training a week later, Aaron cleaned up in the DZ shower hall and headed to Mayberry Market on his way home. Moments later, he wheeled the buggy to the meat section. An idea struck. He punched in his home number. "Yeah, Mina? Ask Sarah if she has plans for dinner. Tell her I'm asking."

After what sounded like a scuffle, Mina came back on the phone, a little more breathless than before.

"Everything all right there?" Aaron asked.

Female shrieking sounded in the background.

Aaron paused his cart. "Please tell me the boys don't have her locked in the coat closet."

Mina laughed. "No, no. We're playing hide and seek. Sarah has no plans for dinner. I tol' her you invited her to stay and she said yes!"

"You sound entirely too enthused about this, Mina." And the fact that her excitement caused her accent to thicken both clued in and amused him.

Aaron bit back a chuckle at another female shriek and the sound of his twins' exuberant laughter.

"I have to go! Must move tables and chairs back before you get home, then I'll cook for us, something nice, okay?"

Move the tables and chairs back? Never mind. He didn't want to know.

"Mina, listen, don't cook. You've worked overtime as it is lately with the boys. Take the night off and simply enjoy dinner on me."

"You serious?"

"You bet."

"Ah, you grilling I hope?"

"Planned on it."

"Chicken? Shrimp? Steak? What?"

"Definitely steak. And salt-baked potatoes. And fresh sweet corn on the cob, dripping with butter."

Across the line, Mina grew silent a moment, certainly a rare occurrence, no doubt pondering his words.

He smiled to himself as he put a package of steaks in the cart and pushed it toward the dessert section. "Although I need you to look up a recipe for me."

"*Si,* anything. Just say."

"Pumpkin pie." After she recited the recipe, he reached for the Cool Whip topping. He wanted to make this dinner special. For at the end of it, he'd welcome Sarah on as their new nanny.

He knew in his heart this was right.

As long as her background check came back clean, his boys had their nanny.

The house was big enough that she could have all the privacy in her downtime that she desired. She'd mentioned needing every other Saturday night off. That worked well since he wanted to spend solo time with the boys, too. And Mina would remain, so their arrangement wouldn't compromise Sarah's reputation.

This felt right.

And if he was hearing God correctly, he was checking into Sarah's past for nothing. He needed to call his sister. A government skip tracer, Ashleigh had open access to sensitive information and would be able to use her investigative experience to tell him. Which reminded him… Aaron dialed Ashleigh. No answer. He waited for her voice mail.

"Yeah, Ash? I've got someone I need you to run for me. Name's Sarah Graham." Aaron recited other info about Sarah that would ease Ash's background search, then hung up. Sure, the agency would have run a check. But Ash could dig deeper.

Though he had no reason to believe Sarah was anything but safe, he had to be sure for his boys. He'd learned the hard way that looks could deceive. But rarely did first impressions. And something told him God had sent this woman as a gift. She'd be good for the boys.

Maybe good for you, too, another mind-whisper trailed.

Aaron paid for his groceries and headed home, feeling a rush of anticipation. It turned to laughter as he walked past the living-room window. All of his house's inhabitants' torsos tilted side to side as their feet took them in wild, wacky circles. And of course, Sarah led the pack.

Aaron viewed his furniture, pushed to the sides of the room where the foursome danced to what sounded like the Hokey Pokey. And he knew with certainty his carefully ordered life was about to unravel.

For good.

Good!

Aaron didn't seem fazed about the misplaced furniture or up in arms over the chaos she'd created in every corner of the room. Something twinkled in his eyes and a smile dawned at the twins dancing. That was good, right? The rest of his face remained unreadable, however.

Sarah dialed down the stereo volume. "Boys, Daddy's home."

That's all it took to rocket-thrust the twins toward the door. Something jolted in Sarah's mind at her own wording. "Daddy" sounded much too much like something a wife would say to her children about their father. Maybe Aaron hadn't noticed.

Then again, according to the way his chin slowly rose as he studied her, maybe he had. As the boys rushed across the floor toward him, he set down the grocery sacks and knelt for the impending double impact, but continued to watch her. She made herself busy picking up stray toys. After all, she far from deserved a man like Aaron.

The usual militantly focused look in his eyes

softened as he nestled one twin in each arm. "Hey. Did you guys miss me or something?"

Melt!

How could they not?

She did.

Her own thoughts caused her cheeks to burn.

"Yes. You were gone a long time." Bryce's bottom lip quivered. "The sky tried to send a storm but Miss Sarah prayed it away."

Aaron eyed her for a long while. The longer he looked the more his eyes sparkled with softness. "Did she now?"

Braden nodded. "Uh-huh, but I wouldn't have been scared."

"Why's that?"

"She made a tent of blankets near the couch for naptime and let us sleep in the same room with her. We pretended to camp."

Aaron held her gaze, approval evident in his eyes. "That was nice of her."

She busied herself straightening the room, mostly to escape the potency of his mesmerizingly pleased expression.

You're acting like a freak of nature! He's just your boss! Well, almost her boss. Hopefully.

"Thanks for making a game of it," Aaron said, coming close. Closer than a boss would.

She remembered to breathe. "No problem. It was fun for me, too." Grocery sacks lifted, she headed for the kitchen.

Following, Aaron bit back a laugh.

"What's so funny?" Sarah set the bags on the counter.

"Images of you performing silly dances when I walked up. You seem quite proficient at the Hokey Pokey."

Heat blasted her cheeks but she laughed regardless. "You can see in the windows?"

He grinned. "Very clearly."

"Maybe we should keep the blinds closed, then." She adjusted her collar and turned her attention to the groceries. His hand brought up a package.

Sarah blinked. Joy streaked through her. "Steak?" It came out as a squeak.

Aaron pulled more items from the sack. "And salt-baked potatoes. And corn on the cob that will drip with—"

"Butter." She rose on her toes and clapped as he held it up. Then grew serious. "I don't know what to say, Aaron."

He moved close enough for her to catch whiffs of cologne that were entirely too enticing.

"Just say you'd still like to be our nanny. Because if you do, this is a welcome-to-our-home celebration dinner, complete with pumpkin pie and two tubs of Cool Whip."

She shrieked and started to hug him, then, mortified, caught herself. She jolted inches away and stuttered nonsense. "I—I'm so sorry. I'm just so thrilled about this and I didn't mean to nearly attack you there."

Sarah glimpsed a part of Bryce in Aaron's shy grin.

He shrugged. "It's okay. Mina does it all the time. She comes from a family of huggers. I wouldn't have thought anything of it."

Yet his uncertain eyes said something altogether different and it scared her absolutely to death. Because the flint of longing in her heart matched the strike of yearning in his eyes the moment she'd nearly thrown herself at him in her excitement over the job.

Wait. He had mentioned Mina's family. Yet not his own. Why?

This man was larger than life. An intentional hero. Internationally esteemed. This silly zinging and these wayward thoughts would wear off in time. They would. They had to. For no upstanding, respectable man in his right mind would want to entangle himself with a woman harboring her past.

"Sarah, one more thing." He'd turned serious.

Her heart thudded. *Oh, no. He knows.*

"I'm very uncomfortable with you living at the roach motel."

She breathed more freely. "I've seen no bugs. Except moths near the streetlight."

"I'm talking human roaches. Being right off the interstate, that's a pay-by-the-hour motel. You know that, right?"

"Pay by the—" She gulped.

"So I was thinking you could go ahead and move into the house. If, after the probationary period you or we feel the job isn't right for you, we can rent you the pool house cottage. It's on our property but twice the size of the motel room."

She nibbled her lip. "Speaking of roach motel, uh, someone broke into my car and stole my CDs."

Aaron pivoted to face her. Concern slid into his features. "Did you call the police?"

"Yes. Filed a report. They said it was probably one of the many juvies in the neighborhood."

"So the sooner we move you in here, the better I'd feel about your safety."

"I'm really getting the job?" She pinched herself.

He issued a brief nod.

She resisted the urge to leap and shriek again.

"We could move you in Tuesday."

"Yes. I don't have many possessions."

"Still, I'll come over a little early and bring boxes."

"So this means Wednesday morning I'm officially the nanny?"

Wednesday. His throat closed.

How had he forgotten?

Wednesday would have been his and Donna's nine-year anniversary, had she lived.

God, what does this mean? Anything?

And upon hearing the news, Sarah had almost hugged him. And he'd almost wished she would.

He swallowed hard. Needed to up the ante of vigilance to keep his mental, emotional and physical code of thought and conduct in the realm of employer-employee relationship only. "Yes. Unless something bad shows up on your background check, it's official."

He didn't miss that his words wiped the smile from her face. Why? Doubt crept in.

"Don't look so scared, Sarah. I was sort of kidding about something bad showing up."

She froze. "I thought the agency already ran one."

He nodded and watched her carefully for a reaction. "They did. I'm digging deeper. And further back."

Her face paled even more and her gaze dropped to the counter, where she made her hands busy with opening dinner packages. Fine tremors shook her fingers.

This was definitely a woman harboring secrets.

Or hiding scars.

Or both. Both of which left him unsettled.

"Sarah, if there's something you need to tell me, something that may show up on a decade-old search, I'd appreciate hearing it from you."

As opposed to finding it out on his own. And for his twins' sake, he would. "If you're in some kind of danger—"

"No. That's not it." She brushed a long, beveled wedge of bangs aside and tucked them behind her ear. "I made a series of bad choices my senior year. Graduation night, I was arrested."

Unable to help it, he laughed. "Is that it?"

"No." Her mouth trembled. He felt bad for laughing. "I made a horrible mistake that I have regretted every day since."

"Which tells me you haven't or won't make the same mistake again?"

"That's right. If you want to know details—"

"I'll ask." Something told him to trust her.

She looked at him like he couldn't be serious and it couldn't be this easy. Then deep gratitude settled into her features, which convinced him that whatever she'd done was indeed in her past.

"Do you have any other questions?" Sarah's mouth trembled slightly as she asked. Most people probably wouldn't have noticed. But being a leader who trained military special operatives in detecting microscopic body language cues, he definitely noticed nuances most people didn't.

"Yes, I do have one final question."

Her eyes appeared tremulous, yet she met and held his gaze like a manly handshake. She appeared braver than some of the young airmen coming into Air Force boot camp. His respect for her soared.

She tilted her chin up. "Yes?"

"How do you like your steak cooked?"

A blank, bland expression. Then a few dawning blinks, then relief and gratitude flooded her face. She socked his arm. "Well done."

"Well done?"

She arched a brow. "Is there any other way, Chief?" And he suddenly felt swallowed by a set of eyes so pretty they could make a Navy SEAL swoon. Or maybe it was the spunk in her statement throwing his pulse for a loop.

Or possibly this monster of attraction raring up. A hug certainly would have fed it, regardless of Sarah's intentions. But he hadn't wanted to make her feel bad over a spontaneous and exuberant act of innocence. Innocence that so embodied her, he felt nearly foolish for calling Ash to check Sarah out. The nanny agency would have run a fairly decent background check.

But Ash could dig deeper. Way deeper.

Unfortunately, she was out of the country chasing an international fugitive at the moment. Could be weeks, even months before she'd return, her supervisor had told him when he'd called back after Ash didn't answer his voice mail.

Ash's job posed a danger, but she was careful and good.

Bring Ash home safely.

Until then, Aaron would settle with the agency's background check.

For now.

"It was fun while it lasted," Aaron said to Sarah as he walked her to her car after dinner and a board game with him, Mina and the boys Saturday evening.

Sarah laughed, wondering how much she should razz him over ending his winning streak to her. "Yeah. But I'm sure you'll make a comeback to stomp me the next game."

He opened her car door. "Count on it."

His grin caused her to bump her head on the car frame as she lowered herself to the driver's seat. She winced.

"Ouch." He brushed a hand along the back of her head. "That had to hurt."

"It's okay. I'm pretty hardheaded." No, really she

wasn't okay as long as the deliriously charming man massaged her head.

Maybe he sensed it because he withdrew. "Thanks for sharing game night with us, Sarah."

"My pleasure. Especially the part about beating you."

He chuckled then scanned the seat beside her. "Do you have your backpack?"

She looked around. "Ugh. I think I left it on the coat hook." She reached for her door.

He waved her back. "I'll go get it for you."

Sarah lifted her gaze from its admiration of the powerful legs that took him to the house in a full, fluid sprint.

She eyed her watch. Still early evening. She'd helped Mina with the dishes and still had time to kill before her meeting. With the five-minute drive, she'd have plenty of time to go over her notes.

Not that she'd need them. The speech she was to give tonight at her local AA meeting was written soul-deep into her heart. She'd followed her pastor's suggestion that she contact the local chapter for membership and continue to sponsor and speak at meetings, since her story might prevent others from relapsing. Something she knew, with God's continued help, she'd never do. Plus being a sponsor deepened her commitment.

Though she'd been well on her way to graduating from being a party drinker to a full-fledged alcoholic, everything changed in a bad judgment-instigated instant. The vivid image and sensory memories of striking someone's child at dusk so many years ago superseded any draw that alcohol had on her.

Aaron came back out of the house and jogged to her car. Sarah rolled down the window as Aaron rolled up his sleeves—a quirky thing he did nearly every time he initiated a conversation with her.

"Coming back tonight?" Aaron leaned in her open car window. His nearness put her breathing at risk. Not to mention his eyes looked vulnerable and, dare she say, hopeful?

She hated to disappoint him, but she needed to write her letter and get her other affairs in order before moving in.

Joy consumed her until she remembered that unearthing her past could forfeit her future with this family.

"Unless you think Mina needs help tonight, I'll head back to the motel. Get a head start on packing if you don't mind."

"Sounds good. See you Monday…Nanny." He smiled.

Smiling to match his, she started her car. "Monday it is…Chief. First thing in the morning."

He grinned. "First thing."

Chapter Six

The first thing Aaron noticed when he came down the driveway was all the water. Mud flooded the yard, void of grass.

"What on earth?" Did he have a water leak? He parked his SUV in the usual place, outside the garage, since all of Donna's stuff was still in the garage.

He really needed to clean it out. But hadn't been able to bring himself to go through her things. He honestly wished someone else would do it. But Mina couldn't lift all those containers and boxes. And truthfully, like his boxed grief, he'd rather not reopen it. Pizza he'd picked up on the way home in hand, he trekked toward the back.

Quickening his pace, he stuffed keys in his pocket and followed the downward stream of water. Looked as if it was coming from around the side of the house. Steps later, he heard rounds of raucous laughter floating from the direction the water path trickled. As the source came into view, he slowed.

Sarah and the boys were running through sprinklers. A strange sight given they all had on jeans and long-sleeved shirts beneath—he leaned forward—were those lawn bags? Yes. With arm and head holes poked out.

Fall in southern Illinois was like that. One day he could wear shorts and a T-shirt. The next might require long sleeves, pants and a jacket. Mina had often switched from air to heat the same day.

As he took in the scene at the top of the grassy hill, his steps decelerated even more.

Something shifted inside. His emotion maybe. He realized again that he was staring. And smiling. He didn't care to stop either one. Taking in the hilarious and heartwarming sight of his boys leaping across tiny streams of water caused spontaneous laughter to geyser. Like the parched earth beneath the rhythmically drizzling sprinkler, he soaked in his sons' high-pitched squealing and chortling. Sounds of unbidden fun seeped into his consciousness like the water into their clothes.

Another unexpected emotion emerged at the sights and sounds of Sarah's laughter mingling with Bryce's. Longing. Longing for more. More than what life had been offering him and what he'd been offering it. The want for companionship came out of nowhere. Aaron took a somewhat dazed step as this enchanting, invigorating creature lifted his smaller son and swung his feet across the squirting arches of water. Bryce threw his head back and laughed as hard as Aaron had ever heard him.

The strangest feeling descended.

She completed them.

It both terrified and entranced him.

Bryce laughed again. In the shared moment of exhilaration, Braden spontaneously hugged his brother, something that also happened rarely. Like a button on his iPod, it paused him. As did the scene before his eyes.

It reached in, like soul balm, and touched a part of his heart that hadn't been beating since the day Donna's stopped.

Slowly, he felt that part revive. The part that clung to companionship and had hurled headlong into marriage and fatherhood, with hopes of giving his children this kind of joy.

Only it hadn't happened that way. Loss had vacuumed it from his life. It was all he could do to get through each day and try to force happiness into their home for his boys' sake.

Obviously he hadn't done a good job.

Seeing little Bryce leaping, jumping, running and so carefree with his face alight in joy, and seeing how loving Braden could be when provoked with fun, nearly did him in emotionally. And Sarah's giggles produced the same result. She probably had no idea the miracles God had used her to work in his yard today. And in the souls of his children. Aaron swallowed past a painfully ambivalent lump.

He considered himself a good father. The best. But why hadn't he ever thought to run through the sprinklers with his boys? Something so simple, yet so profoundly fun to them.

He sighed and moved on, choosing to let them continue their carefree play while he checked on Mina.

Once inside, he tapped on Mina's door. "Feeling better?"

She pattered to the door, looking rested and relaxed.

"Yes. I had a headache, so Sarah kindly offered to take the boys outside to play. That way they wouldn't disturb me."

Aaron leaned against the doorframe and folded his arms. "Know what they're out there doing?"

"No telling. That girl loves to take the boys outside for fresh air. I can't take it because of my fall pollen allergies and the sun in summer. Heat intolerance. But more power to her."

"Yeah. It's good for them to be outside. All that solar-induced vitamin D and fresh air is good for the bones and all."

"Not to mention all that fresh laughter is good for the heart and all." Mina eyed him intensely.

"I should be taking them out more. I guess I never think about it. They're always inside."

"Well, your job puts you outside in the elements a lot. It's relaxing to put your feet up inside."

"Still, seeing how much fun they're having out there makes me realize I need to be more vigilant with getting the yard in shape so they can do more outdoor play. Which reminds me—" He tugged on her sleeve and grinned. "Come on. I want you to see this."

Seconds later, after Aaron led her to the garage

window, Mina chuckled with her whole body as she watched the boys and Sarah frolic outside. "They're having a hay day with that sprinkler. I should get towels ready. Sarah just turned off the water hose."

"I saw towels draped over the tree limb there."

"You're right. Smart girl, that Sarah." Mina eyed him cautiously. "And pretty. Even when drenched like a puppy after a bath." Her gaze sharpened.

So Mina had caught him watching Sarah's trek to the tree.

Aaron pulled his gaze from the window. "I need to put this pizza in the house."

Mina's chin lowered. "Don't change the subject, Aaron Michael." She stepped toward him.

He pivoted in a half circle, intent on entering the kitchen through the garage door. Just then he caught sight of Donna's stuff, which took up half the garage. Gut-crushing grief ran across him like a military tank. Pain. Harsh and swift. Too much pain in this room. And too much risk in pondering the possibility of going through it again.

Squeezing the box, he marched up the garage steps toward the house, launching a firm gaze at Mina. "I'm not changing the subject. I'm officially closing it for discussion as of now."

She paused, her smile dissolved.

Remorse hit. Instantly he felt bad disrespecting his elder. He stepped back toward her. "I'm sorry, I—"

She smiled, met him halfway and placed a gentle hand against his cheek. Same way she used to when he'd majorly crashed his bike or wiped out on his skateboard to the point that blood and brag-worthy bruising were involved. "It's okay," she said. "You're not ready. I didn't mean to tease. Forgive me."

Motherly compassion in her face clogged his throat of sound. So he just nodded. And swallowed. But words still couldn't ease past the acidic emotion.

He placed his hand over hers and gave it a good squeeze, hoping to convey his gratitude for all she'd done.

The smile deepened in her eyes and mouth. "You're tough. But sometimes I forget that you're not made of titanium. Come. Let's feed those little water bugs." She took the pizza.

He entered the hallway to greet the boys.

"Daddy!"

"Hey. Hold on." He stepped across trash bags Sarah spread along the floor, probably so they wouldn't track in mud as they ran to hug him.

"Having fun?" Aaron asked Sarah while helping her ready the boys for a warm bath Mina had drawn.

Sarah grinned shyly and pulled off a trash bag she'd placed over her shirt. "Admittedly, yes. I think I had more fun than they did."

Aaron remembered Bryce's carefree exuberance and Braden's uncommon affection. "I don't know. They looked as if they were having a pretty good time themselves. You're good with kids, Sarah."

Was it the bathroom lighting, or did her cheeks tinge?

"Thanks. I hope you're not mad about the yard. I didn't realize it would get so muddy."

"I'm not worried about the yard. I should have planted grass. Flowers. Shrubs. Something. It's just, after Donna died, I guess I sort of let things in the yard go." He eyed it through the floor-to-ceiling windows.

Desolate.

A reflection of how he'd felt inside.

Until recently.

Until Sarah.

Now in the bathroom, she knelt to turn off the water. "That's understandable."

Aaron tossed in two clean washcloths and tried to ignore how much he enjoyed sharing household tasks with her.

She plunged her elbow in the liquid. "Nice and warm but not too hot."

"I like how safety-conscious you are. Most people don't know to use a different part of their body than their temperature-desensitized hand to check bathwater."

"Those parenting magazines in hospital waiting rooms come in handy."

He nodded. "Come on, boys. In you go."

Then something hit him. Why had Sarah spent time in hospital waiting rooms? He studied her.

While she broke into singing silly songs with his boys, Aaron exited the bathroom.

Mina approached with the folded trash bags. "Not a drop of mud anywhere. Just how did she pull that off?"

"I can't imagine." Aaron started to take the pizza to the kitchen.

Mina intercepted it. "I'll take that. You go help her."

"But—"

"No buts. Go."

"—the bathroom is so small."

She grinned like a loon. "I know."

Feeling set up by the woman who'd practically raised him and Ash after their parents had died, Aaron rolled up his sleeves and went to meet his fate.

"Need help?" Aaron stepped inside the bathroom hoping she wouldn't.

Sarah turned to peer at him. "I think I can handle it."

"Well, if I don't assist you, Mina will have my head."

"Well, we can't have a headless Dadsman running around." She scooted over. He knelt beside her on the long bathroom rug. Their elbows kept bumping. And their forearms kept brushing. And they both kept apologizing. And turning red. And the boys giggled. And every time it happened, Aaron shot Mina an accusing look through the door.

She held her head high and met his ire with a level of amused innocence that more than gave her away.

"I think we're about done." Gurgling sounded as Sarah let out the water, much to the protest of Braden. Aaron towel-dried them and their hair, then helped them step into clean clothes.

After Sarah tidied the bathroom, she led the boys into the playroom. She had them start picking up toys. Aaron went into the kitchen to fix the boys plates of pizza.

Everyone gathered around the table and chowed down. The boys headed off to the playroom. Mina headed to the kitchen with Aaron. Sarah entered the playroom looking a little haggard.

He eyed the clock. She'd been working for twelve hours already. No wonder she was showing signs of moving slower.

"Chasing after kids is hard work," Aaron said to Mina.

"Yeah. Whoops, looks like Braden is climbing her like a tree. So we'd best go rescue her before she wises up and flees."

Aaron laughed. "True."

But eyeing Sarah and how she dodged and blocked Braden's roughhousing with tickling maneuvers and boundless energy, he had a feeling this nanny could hold her own. Even with his rambunctious twins. Though he sensed she desperately wanted him and the boys to like her, she hadn't skimped on disciplining Braden when needed.

"A lot of new nannies would have foregone the time-out in order to gain the child's favor," Aaron said quietly to Mina. "That she held the consistency I value and her sons' best interest over her own pleases me."

Mina's head whipped around. Her eyes grew wide. Then she giggled.

Aaron peered down at her. "What?"

"*Her* sons?" Mina's brows shot to the moon.

He felt color drain from his face. "I didn't—"

"You did."

"No, I'm—"

"Yes. You—"

"—quite sure I didn't—"

"—certainly did."

"I'm tired, Mina. Give me a break."

And to his plea for mercy, she guffawed. "Oh, sure. Sure. I'll give you a break. Breaking news, in fact. You. Like. The. Nanny."

"That's not it. It's because military life is so rigid, I need a place to come home to that is a haven. You in conjunction with Sarah will make that possible."

"Smooth move, Chief. But flattery will get you nowhere. You forget I helped raise you. I've seen the lovestruck look in your eyes before."

"Lovestruck? Hardly. Mina, I—"

"Lighten up, Aaron. I'm kidding. You and the boys are practically family. I'd tell you if I had reservations about the nanny."

"Oh, good."

She dipped her head. "Or about your liking her," she mumbled beneath her breath to her pearl button and slunk off.

Aaron stuck out his arm, doing the daddy-seat-belt maneuver, effectively blocking her. "Tell me? You'd chase her off with a lethal wooden spatula is more like it."

Mina smacked at his arm. He dodged.

"Go." She shooed. "Rescue the girl before we lose a good thing here."

"I refuse to analyze what you mean by that," he tossed over his shoulder.

"Suit yourself." Mina gave his back a not-so-subtle shove. "And for the record, I think we have more blessings at work here than we expected."

He'd never expected this.

Aaron eyed the newly planted baby Bradford Pear trees scrolling by as he navigated his SUV down his long driveway toward the house the next day. This landscaping had Sarah's signature all over it. He'd never expected or asked her to do all this, go to all this trouble. Yet gladness filled him that she had. Bags of potting soil and fall chrysanthemums sat near the garage where he parked. Aaron headed inside.

"Daddy!" Braden released Sarah and attacked Aaron's knees with a mow-you-over hug when he set down his rucksack and entered the room.

Bryce followed with slower, quieter steps. "Hi, Daddy. Look what we drawed you." He presented some colored pages.

"Wow. These look like they took a lot of time and effort." Aaron viewed the artsy cluster of scribbles and wished desperately to know what the crayon-scribed objects were.

"They worked on those all day."

"This is awesome, guys." Aaron cast a thankful glance at Sarah. She eyed the wall clock. The gesture reminded Aaron she had a meeting tonight.

Eventually he'd invite her to Joel's weekend cookouts. Aaron wasn't ready for the ribbing he knew would come from the guys if they picked up on his ridiculous attraction to Sarah.

Hopefully, it would pass. The sooner the better.

"Boys, let's pick toys up." Sarah started to help Bryce and Braden collect their toys in the boxes she'd organized.

Aaron reached for her armful of plastic soldiers and zoo animals. "I know you have somewhere to be. I'll finish up."

"I appreciate that." Sarah bid the boys goodbye, then waved at Mina. Aaron walked her to the door. "You want to take a plate of dinner with you?"

"Nah. I'll grab something on the way."

He nodded and watched her leave, wondering where she went every other Saturday night. But it was not for him to ask. None of his business, really. Or was it? Seemed Sarah worked overtime at trying to keep where she went under tight wraps.

Why?

What did she have to hide? Anything?

Sarah's car disappeared from sight, but the image of her sparkly eyes and smile remained etched in his brain.

On his way back into the house, he dialed his sister's number. Again, no answer. He tried her supervisor, who informed him that Ashleigh was still out of the country on a job. Aaron thanked him and hung up, then redialed Ash's number. He'd leave her a voice mail.

"Yeah, Ash? I'm wondering if you got my message

about needing you to run someone for me. Call when you can. You still coming next month for a visit? Hope so. The boys miss you. Love you. Your favorite brother."

Aaron snickered after hanging up. After all, he was Ashleigh's only brother. But they had a back-and-forth teasing about that.

"Who was that?" Mina cut meat into pieces and put them on the boys' plates.

"Ash."

"She's back in the States?" Mina licked her finger.

"No. I'm just giving her a heads-up by voice mail that I need her to run a more in-depth background check on Sarah."

"But you already hired her."

"Yep."

"Meaning what? If something comes up, let her go?"

"If need be." He put green beans on the boys' plates, then set them on the table while the boys washed up in the bathroom.

"I doubt you have anything to worry about. But it's good you're checking, I guess," Mina said.

"Definitely."

Ashleigh, aka A.K. Petrow, or appropriately nick-named by her working peers as "Agent AK-47," was an oft sought-after government skip tracer known to be ruthless, relentless and highly successful in hiding or finding people.

Or in finding *information about* people.

She'd started out as a private investigator before

being hired by the government to pursue criminals who'd fled the country. She also helped people in witness protection programs to disappear from danger. Ash was a master at digging up old dirt and chasing paper trails. Aaron often teased her that "Investigation" was her middle name.

"If there is anything questionable lurking in Sarah's past, Ash *will* find it."

Chapter Seven

Several Saturday mornings later Aaron motioned Sarah to the kitchen then pointed to an emergency number list. "Sarah, I won't be back until tomorrow morning."

He paused to detect her reaction to the fact he'd be gone overnight. Though she'd been working for weeks, she'd never handled the boys at night before.

While he sensed her shift slightly she also nodded immediately after. Though the news certainly surprised her, she handled, and accepted it well. As if she'd have no problem rolling with unexpected changes. Good sign.

"These are phone numbers in case you run into trouble. Mina will be here. In addition, these four women are wives or fiancées of my local Pararescue team. They all live nearby and will be happy to answer any questions you may have. In addition, I'll check in periodically. But if for some reason I can't be reached in the event of an emergency, please call Celia Peña. She's the voice and will notify the rest."

"After I dial 9-1-1, of course." Sarah shifted her faded brown backpack and smiled.

His pulse ramped. "Of course." It took considerable effort to stop looking at Sarah long enough to point out the next set of numbers on the refrigerator. "These are all emergency numbers in Refuge. Police. Ambulance. Fire. Poison hotline, et cetera."

She nodded. "I think we've got it. You have my cell number in case electricity goes out? Storms are in the forecast tonight."

He'd forgotten that. Bryce was terrified of thunder and lightning. How would Sarah handle that? It'd be a good test. Plus, Mina would be here. "I do have your cell number. You have mine?"

"Yes, but I won't call unless it's urgent because I don't want to disturb your work."

"This is the first time I've left them alone at night. Ever. So if they need to call and talk to me, that's fine. You won't disturb my work."

She nodded.

"I guess I should probably also warn you that Bryce is scared of storms."

"What usually works for him?"

Aaron felt his skin flush. "Admittedly, they usually end up in bed with me when they're scared. And I've probably created a bad habit by letting them sleep there. It's a king-size bed, but still. Probably will be a hard habit to break."

"I'm sure we'll be fine. Anything else?"

"Not that I can think of. Mina will show you where

everything for bedtime is." He peered at his watch. Needed to meet Joel and the rest of the team. "I'll see you sometime Sunday."

An hour after Aaron left, the phone rang. Mina answered it.

"What? When?" Mina launched into panicked-sounding Spanish.

"Wait here, boys." Sarah set down her craft items and walked into the kitchen. Something was wrong. She could hear it in Mina's voice.

At her approach, Mina covered the mouthpiece. Tears filled her eyes. "They think Mom's had a stroke."

Sarah closed in, bracing Mina up by the arms as the person on the other end fed her information. The more they talked and the more Mina listened, the more color drained from her face.

"Mina, what can I do to help?" Sarah whispered during a lull in the phone conversation.

"I need to go to the airport." She got back on the phone. More Spanish. Then Mina ended the call and looked at Sarah. "My brother said I need to come right away. But…" Her eyes veered to the boys. Mina looked about to hyperventilate.

"What can I do right now to help get you out the door?"

"Get the kids ready?" She thrust the phone at Sarah. "And call Aaron Michael. Tell him what happened." Spanish. Spanish. Spanish. "I need to go throw some stuff in a bag." Tears streaked down Mina's cheeks as she went through the dining room to her room. Since that was the long way around, she was probably trying to hide her tears from the boys. Mina wobbled around and came back to Sarah. "I'm so sorry you're thrust into this not fully trained yet."

Sarah firmly grasped Mina's shoulders. "Don't even think about that. I'll manage fine."

"Yes." Mina nodded and drew a deep breath. "I believe you will."

They separated and Sarah went to the playroom. "Boys, can you get your shoes on? We're going for a ride." Sarah kept her actions unhurried and her voice calm.

"Where we going?" Braden stood. Bryce blinked.

"To watch airplanes take off. Doesn't that sound fun?"

"Yeah! Airplanes!" Braden zoomed toward the door. Bryce followed.

While they poked and stuffed little feet into shoes, Sarah slipped to the other room and punched Aaron's number. He answered immediately.

"Aaron, the boys are fine. But Mina's brother called from New Mexico. Her mother has possibly had a stroke. Her brother has recommended that Mina fly in right away."

His deep sigh went straight to her heart. "I'll be right there. I'm a ways away."

"How about we meet you at the airport?"

"Even better. You mind driving? Mina might be too upset."

"Sure. Are there extra booster seats somewhere?"

"In the garage. On top of the boxes near the freezer."

"Okay." Phone to her ear, Sarah gathered the boys' coats. She planted two items from their toy box in their pockets.

"Sarah, thank you." Deep gratitude resided in his tone.

"No problem. See you in a few." She ended the call and helped the boys on with their coats. Then she grabbed Mina's rolling suitcase.

"I'll meet you in the car." Mina said on her way to the coat closet.

Outside, Sarah put the suitcase and booster seats in her car, secured the boys in the seats then buckled herself up.

While waiting for Mina, she turned on a kids' VeggieTales song CD and pulled the car around to the front door.

Mina got in and smiled at the boys. Sarah could tell she'd been crying, but a thin layer of face powder probably hid evidence from the boys.

"You going somewhere, Miss Mina?" Braden asked.

"Yes. On an airplane."

"Oh. Can we go?"

"Not this time."

"Next time?"

"We'll see."

"Why are you leaving?" Braden looked fearful as Sarah drove toward the small Refuge airport.

"My mom is sick. I need to go see about her. But I'll be back."

"Oh. My mommy got sick, too. A car wrecked her. She never came back."

Dead silence. Mina and Sarah looked at one another.

So Donna had died in a car accident? Or had she been a pedestrian and hit? Sarah didn't feel right asking, though she'd wondered.

Sarah reached back to pat Braden's knee. "Miss Mina will come back. Until then, I'll keep you company. How's that sound?"

"Good," Braden said, but he still looked fearful. Bryce, completely still and quiet, watched Sarah and Mina carefully.

Time to play the distraction card again. "Hey, check your pockets. There might be a surprise in there." Sarah turned onto the road leading to the airport.

The boys stuffed their hands in their pockets and dug around.

"Yay! My airplane," Braden exclaimed.

"Yay! My helichopper!" Bryce said and grinned.

"Copter!" Braden corrected.

"Ah-ah-ah. What did we talk about?" Mina said to Braden with firm tones. "We don't criticize our brother. We build him up and give him compliments. Say you're sorry."

"You're sorry," Braden said to Bryce.

"No, tell Bryce *you* are sorry."

"But I'm not."

"Braden Micah Petrowski. Apologize. Now."

Braden scowled at Bryce. "Sorry."

Mina passed Sarah another look. And they both laughed. Braden didn't look or sound at all sorry.

Bryce, thankfully, was too busy lifting his "heli-chopper" to notice.

Aaron was already at the airport when they arrived. He took Bryce from Sarah, who carried both boys, one in each arm for time's sake.

Aaron put his other hand around Mina's waist. The love between them was tangible and made Sarah miss her parents. She'd never lived this far from them and hadn't gotten used to not being able to just drive across town and visit when she wanted.

"I got it, Mina," Aaron said as he paid for Mina's ticket. "This way." Aaron directed her toward baggage check-in.

Sarah took Mina's rolling carry-on suitcase and they walked toward the security checkpoint.

"Give hugs and we'll go watch the airplanes take off," Sarah said to the twins, figuring Aaron would want to talk privately with Mina without the boys being there.

After Mina hugged them, she embraced Sarah. "Thank you. You're God-sent, just in time. Take good care of my boys while I'm gone." The words were whispered with heart into her hair. No one else heard. But tears pricked Sarah's eyes at the endearment. Somehow she knew Mina meant more than just Bryce and Braden when she'd admonished her to take good care of the boys.

"I will. Promise," she whispered back and squeezed

Mina's shoulders. "I'm praying for you, your mom and your family."

Mina nodded and blinked back tears.

Sarah did, too. Though she'd only known this family a little while, she'd come to care deeply for each of them. Partly because God had endowed her with compassion as she'd poured herself into avidly praying for them. And partly because there was a lot about them to love.

"Shall we go?" Sarah took the boys' hands and led them toward the floor-to-ceiling windows where planes could be seen taking off and landing.

"Thank you," a deep voice vibrated over her shoulder several plane landings later.

Aaron.

And he was so close that his breath disturbed tiny hairs on her neck. Heat climbed her face and rested in her cheeks.

He'd undoubtedly only leaned in so the boys wouldn't hear.

Why did the innocent closeness upend her so?

And worse, make her wish for closer, longer contact?

"I hope her mom will be okay," Sarah said in low tones while the boys watched a small airplane taxi down a runway.

"Me, too." His hand rested on her lower back. "Ready to get back home?"

The startle in Sarah's eyes matched how he felt inside. Home.

He meant *his* home. But technically it was now her home, too. Just not in the sense his words had made it sound. Furthermore, he didn't know if she'd startled because of how he'd phrased it, or because he'd put his hand to the small of her back without thinking. This attraction and strengthening emotional attachment was just plain awkward. He'd figured once the newness of knowing her wore off, the fizz would fade.

He couldn't have been more wrong.

"Daddy, can I ride with Miss Sarah?" Bryce asked.

"Sure."

Braden looked at Aaron. "I'll ride with you so you don't get lonely."

Aaron laughed and shuffled fingers through his hair. "Thanks, buddy."

"I know we talked about me going to Kentucky to visit my folks this week. Will you need me to stay?" Sarah took Bryce's hand as he clasped Braden's. The foursome exited the airport.

"Yes. More than ever now that Mina will be gone."

And now, more than ever, Aaron realized God might have sent Sarah. *If so, Your timing is perfect.*

Thankfulness for her dependability and ability to handle swift changes swarmed him. *Thank You for sending this nanny.*

Sunday Aaron returned in time to take the boys to church. "Thanks for getting them ready. Sure you don't want to go?"

"Not today." She set about washing breakfast dishes. He'd called to check on her frequently last night. She'd done fine with the nighttime routine and thankfully the storms had missed them.

On the way home from church, Aaron called Sarah. "Hey, why don't you meet us outside in a few minutes? I thought we could take the boys to the park. Weather's supposed to get testy next week again."

"Sounds fun. The park, that is, not the storm." She laughed at herself. "I'll meet you at the end of the drive."

After picking up Sarah, Aaron whipped the car into the market on Mayberry. "I thought we'd get sandwich stuff. Have a picnic."

Sarah helped Braden from the car as Aaron assisted Bryce. "Which park?"

Aaron lifted Bryce over his shoulders. "Haven Street. Been there?"

Sarah held Braden's hand as she kept pace with Aaron. "Yes. I like to jog around the walking track."

They gathered items for a picnic, then checked out. Once at the park, Aaron grabbed the bags and helped the boys from their booster seats.

Braden sped out, but Bryce immediately dropped to his knees in the car.

Aaron sighed. "Oh, no. Not again." He'd hoped Bryce had gotten over the imaginary…*friends*… stage.

Sarah watched Bryce carefully as he scrounged around plucking invisible items from the floorboard. Sarah looked at Aaron. He averted his gaze, trying to decide whether to let Sarah know about Bryce's imaginary feathered friends, or let her discover it on her own.

She came around to his side of the car and took the bags from Aaron.

Bryce, holding tightly to the bundle of nothings in his arms, scrambled out of the car.

Good. No geese missing from Bryce's imaginary gaggle today.

Bryce bent over and helped invisible stragglers along.

Sarah looked at Bryce oddly and sent another questioning look to Aaron.

He cleared his throat and slowed his steps so Bryce wouldn't hear. "Uh, most kids have imaginary friends. Not Bryce. He, uh, seems to, uh, have an imaginary gaggle of geese."

Her hand went to her mouth and her steps paused. A funny sound came out of her.

"It's okay. Go ahead and laugh. I suppose it is pretty bizarre."

Bryce made motions with his arms and mouthed commands at various spots the ground.

"Apparently a couple of his geese have trouble minding."

Sarah giggled. "Is that so?"

"Yes. He knows when one is missing. Or misbehaving. There's at least one feathery reprobate in the bunch. Sometimes things get blamed on the geese that I think a certain shy twin did instead."

Sarah laughed outright.

She'd never heard anything so silly. Or endearing. "So, is this something you play along with? Or do you downplay it?"

"His pediatrician says it's a phase. That there's no harm in letting him believe. But sometimes the geese get unruly—to a point that I have to step in and moderate or referee." Aaron looked mildly disturbed even discussing the notion.

She eyed Bryce. "He has an imagination out of this world. I think it's good to let him stretch his creative wings."

Aaron lifted a playful brow and set out the sandwich stuff on a picnic table. "Pun intended?"

"Maybe." Though Sarah wanted to laugh, she tried to keep a straight face as she watched Bryce run around with his imaginary feathered friends.

"Boys, time to eat."

"Aw! We wanna play!" Braden struck a gunfighter pose, only without the gun.

"Yeah." Bryce tried his best to imitate Braden's stance.

Aaron laughed. "You can play more after you eat."

"Aww, Dad, a few more minutes?"

"Okay. If you do as we say the rest of the day."

Do as we say. We. Of course he meant him as the dad and her as the nanny. Shame on her heart for speeding up and suggesting a family, parental we.

Aaron broke out the lunchmeat and put thinly sliced turkey and ham on whole-wheat hoagies. Sarah added mustard to Braden's bread and mayonnaise to Bryce's. She also put provolone on Bryce's and Colby jack cheese on Braden's.

Silence and lack of movement at her side let her

know Aaron was watching her. She looked up, arrested by the intent look in his eyes. Meeting his gaze seemed to snap him out of whatever held him deep in concentration.

His motions slowed and his gaze dropped to the spread of food on the table. "You seem to have picked up pretty quickly on their likes and dislikes." He plucked baby carrots from a bag, washed them with bottled water and garnished the boys' plates with them.

"Yeah. For the most part, they're easy to please. As are you."

He moved close enough that warmth radiated off his skin. Came from his eyes, too. "That so?"

She nodded and crunched into a carrot stick, mostly to distract herself from his dimples when he smiled as if he liked her.

"That surprise you?"

"What?" Swallow! The carrot nearly lodged. Never mind. He couldn't read her thoughts. Right?

What had they been saying, anyway? Oh, him being easy to please. Right. "With your military status and bearing, uh, yes. I admit I was nervous about meeting your expectations." She handed the boys antibacterial wipes as they came to the table.

"But you don't meet my expectations."

She felt color drain from her face.

Aaron reached over and plucked a carrot from her plate. "You exceed them." He grinned. She jabbed his ribs with her elbow and helped seat the boys.

Paper plates distributed and everyone seated, Aaron eyed the boys. "Who wants to say grace?"

Braden's hand shot up. "Me, me, me!"

"Okay. Bryce, your turn next time, okay?"

Happy-go-lucky, easygoing Bryce nodded then bowed his head.

"Dear Lord, thank You for, um, the park. And for the day. And for us coming to the park. And for, um, Miss Sarah. And that Daddy found a nanny for us. And who helps Mina. And thank You for everyone in the world and, except the bad people, and thank You for Aunt Ash and for allll the toys she brings us, and thank You for the… Bryce! You're not supposed to eat yet!"

Bryce slipped his sandwich back to the plate. Sarah put her hand to her mouth and peeked through folded fingers.

"And thank You for the food. Bless it in Jesus' name, Amen," Aaron finished for the good of humanity, lest Braden go on saying grace for days.

"Anyone up for Frisbee?" Sarah said, rising, after everyone finished eating.

Aaron rose. "Let's be on teams. You take Braden. I got Bryce."

They retreated to an open area of the park that was surrounded on two sides by several stands of trees, which sprinkled their way into a forest. Normally one couldn't see very far into it, but since most of the leaves had fallen, much of the woods was visible.

Sarah jogged with Braden to one end of the open area as Bryce and Aaron situated themselves on the other end. Sarah flung the Frisbee toward Bryce. Aaron helped him with the catch then tossed it back toward Braden. After several more times of the adults throwing gentle tosses of the Frisbee to the boys, Sarah threw Aaron for a loop by flinging it over Bryce's head at him. Aaron ran backward and caught it. The challenge in his eyes told her she'd better run long because he was gonna return the favor.

Whoosh!

Man! He put the elbow grease into that one! Sarah jogged backward and thought she had it. Whump!

Nope. Her foot caught an upturned tree root and she went down. Laughing, but she went down nonetheless.

Aaron, not laughing, was by her side in a split second. "You okay?"

She raised her face, chuckled. "Yes. My pride is the only casualty."

He chuckled, too, and grasped her hand to pull her up. Once up though, he didn't quite let her go, leading to a brief, odd moment where they stared at one another before their hands parted.

Sarah didn't have to hear his words or look in his eyes to read his mind. Neither of them had wanted to let the other's hand go. The moment lasted long enough for the boys to notice, because they giggled.

Exhilaration rushed through Sarah like the Frisbee sailing across the air. She should *not* be this kind of

happy around Aaron. She should *not*. She should *not*.
She should *not!*

But her heart wasn't quite convinced.

After more Frisbee time and the laughter that came
with it, Braden tugged on Sarah's sleeve. "I gotta go!"

"Okay. Do you know where the bathrooms are?"

He nodded toward a building twenty feet away.
Though the door was in plain sight, Braden hesitated
and peered at Sarah with a vulnerability she wasn't accustomed to seeing in the rough-and-tumble brother.

She stepped toward him. "Want me to go with you
and wait outside the door?"

Relief slid into his features. "Yes, please." Raising
her arms toward Aaron, Sarah cut her fingers into the
palm of her hand to make a *T* as in "time-out" and
took Braden to the restroom. Aaron continued to toss
the Frisbee around with Bryce.

Once back, they played catch with a small foam
football. Sarah could tell everyone was having fun. She
knew she was. The boys looked nearly worn-out,
though. "Guys ready for something to drink? I made
lemonade."

"With sugar?" Aaron asked.

She averted her gaze. "You don't have to drink it."
Was he mad? She slid him a slightly anxious glance.

Only to discover his full-on smile. The kind of
smile that could make a girl's feet and pulse trip all
over themselves.

"Since he asked and I promised, I'm going to push
Braden on the swings."

"I think Bryce is in his own world." Sarah eyed the more creative brother, who was occupying himself in the sandbox.

Nodding, Aaron stepped away. The air grew a lonely kind of cold beside her. She hadn't realized he'd stood that close until his leaving left a void that left her irked that she'd even noticed it. Or Aaron's smooth strides across the grass. She redirected her attention to making dessert, which was fruit salad. That is if she could remember the difference between mustard and mayonnaise with the distracting hunk-of-man around. Ugh! She spooned the squirt of mustard out of the diced fruit, tossed it in the trash and started over, this time with the *correct* ingredient: the mayonnaise.

After eating dessert and letting the boys play some more, Aaron looked at his watch, then the sky. "Getting cloudy. I suppose we should get them home."

Sarah helped Aaron gather trash. While they tag-team cleaned the area, the boys climbed in antlike frenzy all over the playground equipment. As if they sensed the time to leave drew near and wanted to seize every last second of play.

"Heard from Mina?" Sarah asked, hoping everything was okay.

"Last update, her mom stabilized. Mina hopes to be home in a few days. Which reminds me, I wanted to thank you for jumping in with both feet."

"No problem." Sarah walked toward the twins.

Aaron waved them over. "Boys, time to go."

After the usual moaning and groaning, they slogged over.

At the car, Aaron lifted them onto the running board. Sarah helped buckle one and Aaron the other.

Then Aaron shut the car door.

Bryce let out a blood-clotting scream and pounded the window. "No! Daddy, they're not all in!"

Sarah let out a grateful breath. With that racket, she'd thought Bryce's fingers got slammed in the door.

Aaron reopened the door. "Come on. Shoo. Get in." He motioned his arms repeatedly toward the running board until satisfied all of Bryce's "friends" were in. Then went to close the door again.

"No, we're missing one!" Bryce insisted.

Aaron dipped his head and rubbed his forehead with his fingertips and mumbled something about not knowing which was more ridiculous…the fact that his son had an imaginary set of geese or that Aaron was actually standing here taking time to herd the stragglers of the gaggle into the car.

Aaron got in and started the ignition.

"No! Daddy, they're not buckled!"

Aaron dipped his head. Put the car back in Park. Turned to face Bryce. "They're all buckled."

"No! No, they're not! Sadie and Shy and the rest are but not Gretchen and Breeber and Gidget and Magnum."

"They have names?" Sarah asked.

"Yes." Aaron leaned back and pulled the seat belt over absolutely nothing in the center seat and clasped it.

Sarah tried hard to stop the laugh from blowing out, but it was no use.

Aaron sent her a smirk. "Sure. Go ahead. Laugh your head off."

Sarah wasn't sure which was funnier, Aaron actually buckling in the imaginary geese, or his exasperation at doing so. Or in the whole situation in general.

"So, how many does he have?"

"Um, two sets of twelve. Plus three."

"Over two dozen geese? Twenty-seven. All named?"

"Yes." Aaron's mouth twitched.

"So, what are their names?"

"Breeber, Sadie-girl, Shy-shy, Miss Lyssa, Magnum, Eno, Randa who has an alias of Randy, Lil' Nell, Devan, Harley, Jewel, Janae-nay, Maddie, Curtis-the-robot-goose, Joshy, Hope, Samara, Katie, Toni, Danny, Gretchen, Amanda-blue, Aye-aye, Gidget, Dandy-Brandon, Hannah and…Cricket."

"A goose named Cricket?"

"Yes." Aaron's ears turned red. "And he most often seems to be the troublemaking one. He likes to peck at everything. And he constantly runs off and we have to go look for him. And of course there's Shy-shy, who is apparently addicted to pickles."

"A goose addicted to pickles?" Sarah giggled. "I'm not sure which is stranger, that he is so acquainted with his double dozen imaginary geese, or that you actually have all their names and personalities so valiantly memorized."

"And their ranks."

"Ranks?"

"Y-yes." Aaron's mouth twitched a few more times. "Apparently, they're military birds by nature. Except Magnum. She's a—a rather *assertive* police goose." At his own words, Aaron shook his head. Then finally broke down and started laughing with her at the sheer absurdity.

Bryce was too busy scolding the insubordinate birds to notice. Sarah sneaked a peek at Aaron. He was unbelievably handsome when he laughed. And the more he laughed the more she wanted to watch and hear him laugh some more.

It was good to see him let loose like this.

Not so good that she couldn't tear her eyes away. Or keep her heart from wishing for more times like this with him.

Humor sparkled in outrageously gorgeous eyes and dimples deepened around a mouth that had suddenly become overwhelmingly enthralling.

Hopefully he was too busy chuckling over Bryce's geese to notice that she was studying him.

Aaron stopped at the gas station on the way home.

She got out of the car to wash the windshield and talk to him while he pumped the gas.

"Yo, Chief," a deep voice called behind them. A voice that carried her right home—the man had her same Kentucky accent—a voice that caused a foreboding chill to dance to the tune of dread up her arms.

They turned around. A tall man dressed in a police

uniform approached from a cruiser marked with a Refuge Police logo. He waved.

Aaron set the gas hose lever to auto-fill and faced the officer. "Hey, Stallings. How goes it?"

"Fine. You?" He eyed Aaron then Sarah then Aaron. A curious gleam entered his silvery-blue eyes. Eyes she'd seen somewhere before.

"Fine." Aaron turned toward her. "This is Sarah. She's our new nanny. Sarah, this is Officer Stallings. One of Refuge's finest on the force."

He looked so familiar. Why did he seem familiar? Cold fear clawed at her throat, making words a struggle. "N-nice meeting you."

"Pleasure, ma'am." Stallings reached out his hand and eyed her intently. "Do we know each other?"

Sarah gulped. "I don't think so."

Aaron straightened. Which was when she realized she was still shaking her head vigorously.

Stallings's head tilted the slightest bit. Not with suspicion as much as trying to figure out where he knew her from. "Because you look vaguely familiar."

"I probably just have one of those faces."

"No, I'm sure we've met prior. Where you from?"

"Kentucky."

"Which part?" His forehead creased.

Now she felt interrogated. Though he probably didn't intend it that way. She put the windshield squeegee back in its water bucket, then used a cloth to wipe her hands. Mostly to stall.

Aaron looked from one to the other.

"N-near Paducah."

A slow dawn crested along Stallings's features. He nodded. "Maybe we ran into each other in town. I worked there for a time." He looked from her to Aaron and back. His face became unreadable. "Folks have a nice day."

Aaron studied Sarah long enough to let her know he recognized that Stallings had rattled her.

She forced a smile and faced him. "Shall we head back?"

Slowly replacing the gas hose, Aaron nodded. But didn't smile. He looked vaguely disturbed as he watched Stallings retreat. Stallings kept looking back, which didn't help. And maybe because of fear, she was exaggerating all this.

She could have met Stallings in a Kentucky diner for all she knew. After all, he hadn't said he'd worked as a police officer in Paducah.

Lord, don't let seeds of doubt plant in Aaron's mind, or mine about his hiring me. I know what I was. But I know who I am now in You. Your opinion is the one that matters. I place this in Your hands. And God help me if he finds out my past before I have courage to tell. Or if he requests to know my past before I'm ready to reveal it.

Chapter Eight

What was it?

Every time Aaron looked at Sarah, he wondered. What was that weirdness surrounding Stallings the day before? Anything?

Or was his imagination simply pulling double duty?

"Mina will be home day after tomorrow," Aaron said to Sarah, up early as usual on Monday morning.

She stood at the stove attempting to turn a glob of what looked suspiciously like eggs. A plate of whole-grain bread sat ready to go into the toaster. Fresh-squeezed orange juice beckoned a drink. Turkey bacon sizzled on a back burner, igniting his hunger.

That she'd even try at all stirred appreciation. He stepped over beside her and started dropping bread into the toaster. When she didn't speak, he intentionally nudged her elbow with his.

"Impressive spread considering you're not keen on cooking."

She looked up, seeming surprised at his nearness and proving she was deep in concentration with her duties. Or, according to the telltale circles beneath eyes, not as awake as usual, deep in thought about something. Yesterday?

"Thanks. But don't be impressed until you actually know you can stomach it." She laughed but the joy didn't quite touch her eyes. Something troubled her. Something more than the eggs she was about to burn.

"Can I help?" He turned the burner heat down.

She nodded and moved aside to let him show her.

He'd prayed last night about the park episode and concluded that Stallings had mixed her up with someone else. She'd admitted she'd made dumb mistakes in her youth that she wasn't proud of. Who hadn't? He certainly wasn't proud of sloughing away his first two years in college.

His gut told him to trust her. And he always trusted his gut if he was staying strong with God through prayer and worship.

Sarah peeled off Mina's apron and draped it over the back of the barstool. "Where are the boys?"

"Still asleep." He scooped scrambled eggs onto a serving plate.

Sarah eyed the clock. "Really? Wow."

He motioned to the bacon he was turning. "Would you like to eat breakfast with me?"

"Sure. Do the boys need to be woken up?"

"No. Please, no." Aaron laughed. He drained the bacon and peered over his shoulder. "Late night last night. Braden was in rare form. And Bryce acts like he might be coming down with something. In addition, his geese are in a tizzy."

Sarah laughed and pushed up her sleeves while eyeing the spread of food on the counter. "What can I do to help now that the real chef is thankfully on duty?"

"Brave the toast?" He'd let her take that over. Anything to boost her confidence.

"Can do." She grabbed the bread.

Aaron seasoned the eggs.

"You're a good dad," Sarah said while they worked side by side. She reached up to the cabinet to pull out a stack of plates. It was too tall to reach two plates from the top, so she grabbed more. They were so heavy she looked to be struggling.

Aaron melted at the compliment and at her scent as he moved behind her and lifted his arms above hers to support the plates wobbling in her arms. "Thanks, those are heavy."

"Yeah," he said. And so was the feeling of domestic togetherness that suddenly pounced on him as they lowered the tower of plates together to the counter.

"I suppose I should put some of these plates away. It's not like we have people over for dinner."

Sarah turned and he realized how close they were. And that he still had his arms braced around her on the counter, yet they didn't touch. Her eyes widened, causing him to realize that, though innocent, things suddenly seemed romantic. He took a polite step back.

But an image of him kissing her streaked across his mind. Would have been a prime opportunity.

"You could, you know," she said softly, lifting her head to peer in his eyes.

"What?" His throat dried. Until his mind righted itself enough to realize her words were about having people over for dinner and not in answer to his wandering thoughts about kissing her.

"Oh, right." Have people over. "Maybe I'll let you and Mina plan that after you meet my friends." He turned off the burner beneath the bacon. Wished this sudden sizzle of attraction flaring for Sarah could be so easily extinguished.

He had no business thinking of her that way. None. Nor entertaining ideas of kissing her.

"Sure we shouldn't wake the boys up to eat?"

He shook his head. "I have a feeling your day's already going to be challenging enough."

"Are they grumpy when they get up?" She helped him carry breakfast to the dining table.

"Grumpy is putting it mildly. Tearing through the house screeching like *Jurassic Park* dinosaurs is more like it." Laughing on the last words, he set his plate and himself across from her.

"Let's pray." He took hold of her hands and prayed over the meal. He enjoyed moments of talking with Sarah and sensed she did, too. Her companionship was a blessing. But he needed to be careful that didn't become the focus of their relationship.

After a half hour, the boys came downstairs and

joined them for breakfast. Aaron tried to shake off the feeling that they seemed like a family. Before Aaron's parents had died, when they weren't flying supplies to missionaries, they would make it a point to sit down as a family at mealtime.

After eating, the boys went to the playroom. Sarah started to the kitchen with dishes.

"I'll get that." Aaron reached for the bacon pan.

"Thanks. You don't have to help." Sarah rinsed dishes and set them in the dishwasher.

"I enjoy it."

She shut the water off and eyed him funny. "Washing dishes?"

"Not necessarily that. I like sharing tasks."

"I like for you to be able to relax while you're home."

He moved closer so they stood side by side at the sink. "I meant that I like sharing tasks…with you."

"Oh." Her cheeks tinged.

"Besides, talking to you relaxes me." Aaron set the pan in the sink. Their forearms brushed; their motions paused but the contact remained. And he couldn't be so sure they hadn't intended it to.

Her blush deepened but she met his gaze. "I'm glad."

Whew! Was she ever glad for recessed lighting. It would better camouflage the burn she felt in her cheeks.

Aaron looked at his wristwatch. "Think you'll be fine by yourself all day? It'll be a late night for me. I may not be home before you have to put them down."

Sarah looked at him sideways and smirked. "'Put them down' makes it sound like a tranquilizer gun is involved."

Humor broke out over his face and he laughed, something she'd noticed he'd been doing more of since she'd gotten to know him better.

"I meant putting them down to bed."

She smiled. "I know." She turned toward the playroom. "Boys, come tell Daddy bye."

"Have a great day, Sarah," Aaron said afterward and stepped toward the open door. And it didn't escape her notice that he let his gaze linger longer on her today.

Her cheeks flamed again. She dipped her face before he could see. "I plan to."

"If they give you any problems, call my cell."

"I'm sure they won't."

"I'm sure they might. In addition to being up late, they were woken up several times because of thunder. Not sleeping well equates to a rough day after."

"Nah. They'll be fine."

"It's not them I'm most concerned about." He paused his exodus and flashed an amused grin, which he quickly covered.

"I'll be fine. I can handle tired little bugs."

Halfway to the SUV, he gave a subdued snicker. At the car door, he turned, face alight with a full-blown grin. "Yeah. So good luck with that." He ducked his head and entered the car with his broad shoulders jerking up and down, laughing like he was having a private joke with himself and drove off still laughing.

Sarah shook her head and tried not to miss Aaron's presence or get heady over remembering the tender moments they'd shared in the kitchen. She couldn't explain it but every time they came in contact, their bond strengthened, as if an unseen hand expedited the closeness.

Hopefully this meant she was meant to be their nanny for good. After all, she didn't deserve a family of her own, no matter how badly her heart cried for it. Her dreams had to be denied. She'd gotten off so relatively easy from a crime that could and should have sent her to prison, that surely the consequence and curse of her sins would be taken out on her own children.

Which is why she refused to let herself be a mother.

She'd only had to do a stint of rehab, community service and probation. That hardly seemed ample for the devastation she'd sown when she'd picked up that wretched bottle and enslaved herself to whiskey. If the courts wouldn't punish her properly, then she'd exact it on herself.

Though her previous pastor had tried to convince her she was twisted up in wrong thinking, she couldn't seem to let herself be free to live without regret or guilt. And certainly not free to be a mother.

Precisely three minutes after Aaron's SUV left the driveway, Braden sped into the dining room. "Miss Sarah! You better come! Hurry!" They rushed to the kitchen.

As soon as she saw Bryce standing on top of the

refrigerator shooing invisible geese, Sarah knew she was in for a challenging day.

Fortunately she was able to coax him down.

Unfortunately a basket of marbles and a tub of pink lemonade powder came down with him. The lemonade lid popped open on impact. As she dropped to catch the scattered, rolling marbles, Sarah's knees crunched into the pink drink dust. She scooped handfuls of marbles until a flash on top of the stairs in the next room caught her eye.

"Braden, what on earth?" She surged to her feet only to find them sliding out from under her. Luckily, she caught herself on the edge of the counter.

Unfortunately she wrenched her back in the process.

"Ow." She abandoned the marble roundup in favor of keeping Supertwin from breaking his neck should he slip.

He clung, grinning, to the outside of the banister, twenty feet in the air. "Boys, please stop climbing." Forget Mina, she'd be the one having a stroke at this rate.

The second she hauled Braden off the stairs, the ominous sound of water rushing over the toilet drove her to the bathroom. Breathless, she screeched to a stop outside the door.

"Bryce, what happened?"

"Uhh-h—" He blinked at the water. Blinked at her. Shrugged.

She sloshed over the flooded floor and shut off the valve near the base of the overflowing toilet.

He stared at ripples of water. "I, uh—I dunno."

"Did you use a lot of toilet paper?"

"I didn't use it. I only flushed it. But water came out and out and out. Braden used the potty last."

After spreading every available towel on the floor to sop up water, Sarah found the plunger. Bryce slunk off.

Clattering, then a horrendous crash sounded from the kitchen. "Oh, no!" Sarah bolted toward the next chaos.

Both boys, surrounded by particles from a shattered vase that looked as if it cost more than her car, pointed at the other twin.

"He bumped it," Braden said.

Tears filled Bryce's eyes. "B-b-but he pushed me into it."

Sarah brushed her hair aside and tried to pretend like her hands weren't trembling and her heart and lungs weren't heaving. How could she get to them without their feet getting cut?

She leaned forward. "Bryce, here." She lifted him across the sea of glass. Then she reached for Braden. Once she had him in her arms, she pivoted to set him to safety. The point she'd earlier strained in her lower back popped as she twisted. "Ahh!" Unbelievable pain seared up and down her tailbone.

"Owhh!" Whatever she'd just done wasn't gonna feel good tomorrow. Hopefully it was just a pulled muscle. Teeth grinding, she set Braden down. Pain streaked across her lower back, causing her to bow over.

She knew better than to twist and lift. Why hadn't

she used better body mechanics? "Oh. Kay. Boys, stay out of this room while I get this cleaned up, okay? In fact, you two owe me a time-out for climbing. So please go sit on opposite ends of the couch until I say you can get up."

Which would be sometime tomorrow at this rate. Ugh. Of course she'd only leave them in a few minutes. Or as long as it took to clean up the dangerous glass.

"Sorry, Miss Sarah," Bryce said, shuffling to the couch.

"Me, too." Bryce plopped himself down opposite Braden.

Nodding, she drew deep breaths and tried to stand. Ignoring how badly it hurt, she used the back of her hand to dab at sweat breaking out over her lip and forehead. Pain. Pain. Pain. She needed an ice pack. But first she needed to pick up this glass.

"Okay, three minutes are up. You can go play now."

After wearing out the broom and dustpan, she checked on the boys in the playroom.

Ice to her back and plunger in hand, Sarah limped to the bathroom, fighting tears and losing. Her back *really* hurt.

After a half hour of *push-slurp, push-slurp, push-slurp,* she knew something was seriously lodged in the commode. Ice had melted in the pack and her back ached something fierce. Every time she moved, her breath hitched at the electrical jolts near her tailbone. She hoped she hadn't caused a permanent injury.

She opened the childproof latch and dug under the

sink until she found drain cleaner. She poured it in, to no avail. She moved to stand. Her back caught, resulting in a moan.

The twins stood at the door with wide eyes.

"Boys, did one of you happen to put something in the toilet besides paper?"

"Daddy said to help you today. And the potty smelled bad," Bryce said.

"What did you put in the toilet, sweetie?"

"Uh, something to make it smell good." His eyes veered toward the back of the toilet. A bottle of air freshener rested there.

"That wouldn't have caused the blockage."

"No, but a candle might." Bryce stuck a finger in his mouth.

Sarah knelt. "Did you put a candle in there and flush?"

Tears filled Bryce's eyes as he quickly nodded.

Sarah sighed and pulled him close. "At least you were honest about it. That helps."

"Are you mad?"

"No. And I'm not going to leave you, either. Is that what you're scared of?" She wiped his tears as he nodded.

After issuing another couple of hugs, Sarah eyed the mess around her, fighting dismay and still overwhelmed. "You boys run along and play. Use the upstairs bathroom if you have to go, okay?" Her back, her back, ow! Her back. She fought to control her breathing. Slowly, she stood straighter. The pain eased substantially. Thank goodness!

They nodded. Braden sped toward the playroom. But Bryce hung around the door. "Miss Sarah?"

"Yes?" She pulled open the cabinet and looked for a plumber's snake. She'd take the toilet apart if need be. If that didn't work, she'd call a plumber. Or Aaron.

"Daddy said to help you with chores. Can I help move Mount Laundry?"

Sarah laughed. Then stopped. Must have moved wrong. Her back hurt, hurt, hurt. *You're being a wimp, wimp, wimp!* she continued to scold herself. Anything to distract from pain and worry over how much that shattered vase cost and the sentimental value attached. "Mount Laundry?"

"Yeah. That's what Mina calls it when we put our clean socks and T-shirts and un-un-matching-a-bells away."

Whether that meant socks that didn't match, or a code word for their underwear, Sarah couldn't be sure. "Unmansionables," Braden corrected.

Resisting the urge to further correct "unmention-ables," Sarah eyed the heaping baskets in the hall across from the bathroom. "Sure. You know where things go?"

He nodded. "I watch Mina all the time. We put the stuff away on shelves we can reach. We get stars on our chore chart."

"Okay. Do you know where your daddy keeps his tools?"

"The basement." Bryce pointed her toward the garage. "The door's in there."

"Why don't you boys sing for me?" If they sang, she'd know where they were and that they were okay.

Sarah searched until she found a plumber's snake. She fed it down the toilet. Every movement caused her back to draw up in pain. The snake didn't cure the clog. She donned a ridiculously huge pair of itchy gloves and took apart the toilet, methodically laying each piece in the bathtub so she'd know how to put it back together.

Something caught her attention. Total quiet. Never a good thing with kids.

She listened carefully. Nothing. The boys' singing had stopped. Only to be replaced with twin "Uh-ohs."

She emerged from the bathroom. A sense of dread overcame her as she went in the direction of the boys. At least her back felt better.

The only sound that she could hear was the washing machine. Which she hadn't started. And which sounded very, very ill.

Opting for a sprint at the thought of the boys starting the washing machine of their own accord, she rounded the corner. "Whoop!" Too fast. Feet flew out from under her. *Whump!* She slipped again onto her back.

She looked at the hall around her. Disbelief rose like the bubbles crawling across the floor. She scrambled to standing and cautiously approached the laundry-room door, under which thick ivory froth oozed.

Bryce and Braden stood frozen to the side.

She jerked open the door. Then slammed it and leaned against it, sliding to the floor. No way. No way did she really see what she thought was in that room. Foamy whiteout.

Total bubbles.

"Boys, what happened? Who turned on the washer?"

Bryce teared up. "I was only trying to help."

"Miss Sarah, he put this in there." Braden pointed at a tipped-over bottle of dishwashing detergent. Industrial-size.

And empty.

"The whole thing?" It was full, last she checked.

He nodded.

"Oh, you didn't use laundry detergent?"

"I—I tried. But the box tipped in. I couldn't get it out."

Sarah pushed open the door to a wall of bubbles.

"So you also used dishwashing detergent?" Trying to keep her voice calm, Sarah tried to walk through the wet haze but the soap stung her eyes. She closed them and tried to shuffle her way, hands waving in crisscross motions before her, toward where she thought the washer was. Her feet slipped. Too late she remembered there was a step down to the washer and dryer. She'd break her neck trying to shut the machine off.

She needed to get rid of some of the bubbles first to increase visibility. She exited the froth and set both boys on the couch for cartoon time. How could she get these bubbles cleaned up so she could safely find her way to the washer and end the siege? She went to the garage and grabbed the wet/dry Shop-Vac. She could suck up the bubbles. She plugged it in and hit the switch, but it wouldn't turn on. She started to try a different outlet but noticed bubbles clinging to the face.

"Oh, no!" What if the outlets had gotten wet? Could that start a fire? Certainly it was an electrocution hazard. Should she call Aaron right now? Maybe she should gather all her facts first. Defuse this situation of imminent danger. Just then Bryce started crying that his geese ran off. Like she had time to chase a gypsy gaggle of something that didn't actually exist.

God, help me.

"Bryce, I'll help you find them in a minute."

But he only looked panicked as he rushed around. "They don't like bubbles! They think it's a monster!"

"They'll be fine." She attempted to console a babbling Bryce with a pat on his head. Unsuccessful. She stepped away from the invisible goose debacle as gracefully as possible and hobbled down the basement steps. Found the breaker box, shutting off the hallway electricity. Bryce's cries escalated to ear-piercing levels. Just then the smoke alarm went off, causing her to remember she had Bagel Bites in the oven.

"Uh-oh. Mi-iss Sarahhhh—"

"I know." She rushed to the smoky kitchen and shut off the oven. Smoke billowed out its edges. She waved the towel to clear the air in front of the smoke detector and turned on the oven light, hoping not to see flames. Ugh! Definite fire in there.

She would. Not. Cry.

"Boys, go to the other room." Smoke billowed from the stove as she covered the tray with a heavy, damp towel to put out the fire. She transferred charred bagels to the sink and ran water over them. Lunch, ruined. Kitchen, nice and smoked. House, saved.

She opened windows to rid the rooms of the smoky smell.

"Miss Sarah, I'm hungry," Bryce said.

Braden stared in the sink. "Miss Sarah, your Bagel Bites look like black little race-car tires."

"I know. You boys go back and sit in the living room and stay away from the smoke." She slapped peanut butter on two pieces of bread, then filled two milk glasses. While they ate, she studied the outlets. Went back down to get an extension cord. She brought it back up and turned on the Shop-Vac. Nothing. Why wouldn't it work? She was afraid to use the regular vacuum on the bubbles because it wasn't a wet/dry vac.

Her eyes lit on the leaf blower. Which didn't need electricity. She could blow a path through the bubbles and get to the washer so the bubble mound would at least stop growing. She found a pair of Aaron's protective goggles and strapped on the leaf blower. "Boys, stay on the couch. I'm going in." She headed toward the bubble monster, now oozing ominously down the hall.

Just then the front door opened.

"Sarah?"

Oh, no.

Aaron must have decided to come home for lunch.

Or to check on her unannounced. Which was fine. Any good parent would. Problem was, the toilet was in pieces in the bathtub. The bathroom floor was still flooded. The obliterated vase was in a pile. The Shop-Vac was dead. The house smelled like a campground and looked like the Milky Way. The hall outlets— soaked. And the laundry room was floor-to-ceiling and wall-to-wall in bubbles. Great. Some nanny she was.

Suddenly, Sarah felt like sitting in the floor and laughing. Or crying. A complete and utter failure.

That was what she was.

Chapter Nine

~⚫

Aaron double-checked his address to be sure he'd walked into the right house. On the same planet. While his yard outside was transforming for the better, the inside was running in the opposite direction. He couldn't believe his eyes.

The downstairs commode was in pieces in the tub. The house reeked of something charred. His boys were wide-eyed and frozen to the couch. And Sarah stood speechless in front of a backdrop of bubbles, dressed in… He blinked.

"My skydiving goggles and a leaf blower?"

Her shoulders lifted in a shrug that never came down. Her mouth wobbled into an almost-smile until a glimmer of threatening tears came to her eyes. She looked as if she could laugh and cry at the same time.

She shut off the machine. "I—I can't get to the washer. The toilet clogged. I tried to fix it. The boys tried to help with laundry and dumped in an entire box plus quite possibly a whole bottle of detergent. I didn't hear the oven timer go off. I might have forgotten to set it. Lunch burned. Then before that there was the fridge incident and the stair escapade and the marble mishap and all the pink lemonade powder and they both played Superman from ridiculous heights. And now the clean laundry is wet, Bryce is wiggy, the geese are gone, the Shop-Vac is dead and the vase ruined."

The stream of words poured out so fast Aaron struggled to keep up much less process it all. He tilted his head. "You lost me somewhere around 'detergent.'"

She blinked exactly twice, then slid to the floor, face in hands. "Who knew? You were right."

Accosted with the urge to laugh, he walked forward. Knelt. "In other words, you had a tough day?"

"I don't understand. I've taken care of many more children than this."

"But I'm guessing that was in a controlled environment for a shorter period of time and with other workers present."

Face rising, she looked so utterly flustered and the scene so unreal, Aaron snickered. He pushed knuckles into his mouth but the laugh escaped anyway.

Her shoulders sank and relief covered her face behind the goggles. "You're not mad?"

"No. This is the most outrageously funny thing I've ever seen." He eyed her getup, then moved toward the laundry room.

She followed him. "So would now be an optimal time to tell you that I think your hall has become an electrocution hazard since water from bubbles got in the outlets?"

He paused, hoping she was kidding. One look at her face told him she wasn't.

"I already turned off the breaker." Sarah turned on the machine, still strapped to her back, to blow a path. Noise blasted out with the forced air. But the bubbles only went to the ceiling and over their heads.

Great idea. Bad aim. Stepping forward, Aaron took hold of the tube that was attached to the blower on her back, and made up-and-down slicing motions. A split surfaced in the middle of the bubble wall. "Stay behind me. I know the way. Be careful of the steps."

"I know. I already found out the hard way."

"There. It's off." Placing the leaf blower tube back in its holder, Aaron turned after shutting off the bubble-spewing washer and bumped something warm. Sarah. She tipped backward. His arms came out to steady her. She must have followed him into the bubbles, which oozed back around them. Blind leading the blind, he helped her out of the froth.

One look at her covered in bubbles and Aaron laughed again. Looking as if she didn't know what else to do, Sarah joined him.

An idea struck. "Hey, boys, bubble fight!" Aaron put duct tape over all exposed outlets, then waved the twins over.

Two seconds later, the boys dove into the white,

bubbly mass. Aaron grabbed handfuls of bubbles and blew them at Bryce. He did it back. Braden flung a handful of bubbles at Sarah. Within seconds, there was a bubble-flinging free-for-all.

Aaron went down, strapped the snow blower onto his back and took Braden on his team. Sarah, armed with the leaf blower, blew bubbles back at them. He and the boys put swimming goggles on, then resumed the fierce bubble fight. Aaron felt like he was having the time of his life. The four of them laughed maniacally as they dodged and swooped through a soapy room of solid white.

The doorbell rang.

Aaron froze. Turned off the blower to be sure. "Expecting anyone?" he asked Sarah.

"No. You?"

He shook his head. Heavy footsteps came across the floor. "Yo, Chief?" Joel called from somewhere outside the bubble zone.

More sets of footsteps. "Petrowski, you here?"

Manny.

Aaron's arms numbed as Joel's voice traveled down the hall. He looked at himself and at Sarah and wondered how many of the guys had decided to drop in unannounced. How would they take this? Moreover, how would he *explain* it?

The urge to laugh or run seized him.

Still wearing the blower, goggles and water shoes he'd slipped on, Aaron girded up his courage and stepped from the effervescent wall of agitated foam.

Joel and Manny stopped in their tracks. Both of their eyebrows slid together on their faces, then rose. They looked at one another. Women's voices came down the hall and around the corner. Amber and Celia, Joel's and Manny's wives, stopped walking and talking midsentence and stared, openmouthed.

Aaron felt completely busted out.

"For sure, the dude's lost it," Manny said, looking Aaron up and down.

Joel stuck a thumb in his pocket and tilted his head. He looked as if he didn't know whether to balk, laugh, leave or help Aaron into a straitjacket.

"What gives, Chief?" Joel asked.

Aaron pushed his goggles onto his head. "Uh, we had a little, uh, there was a, well, see, the washing machine…overflowed?"

Joel's wife eyed the bathtub contents.

"And the toilet. So, uh, Sarah took it apart thinking she could fix it." Aaron shifted beneath Manny's suddenly twinkling eyes.

"Sarah?" Manny peered past him. "Thought we heard a woman's voice."

"We came to see if you needed anything because we know Mina had to leave for a family emergency." Celia stepped in front of him. "So, 'fess up. Who's Sarah?"

"She's the nanny I told you about," Manny said then eyed the wall of bubbles behind Aaron, from which the sounds of Sarah's and the boys' laughter and bubble-frolicking still seeped. "That her in there?"

Aaron's face flamed. "Uh, yeah. She. That would be—"

Celia grinned like a goon and plowed forward. "Yo, girlfriend. Come out. We wanna meet you."

Girlfriend?

Just how did Celia mean that? Some women called one another that as a slangy term of endearment these days. Surely she'd meant it *that* way and not the *other* way, as in inferring Sarah was Aaron's girlfriend.

That would be absurd. Right? Not only was there an age gap, he hadn't a girlfriend since, since, well, Donna.

Aaron leaned far into the froth. "Sarah?"

The leaf blower stopped whirring. Sarah and the boys stepped out, covered head to toe in a hodge-podge of household gear and white, lemon-scented foam.

Joel shifted. "This the new nanny? Or have a ship of bubble aliens seeped through walls to invade your home?"

Celia's eyes rose. "The *nanny?*" She looked Sarah up and down and up and down in quick, bold head motions. "Wow. Cute." She eyed Aaron and waggled her brows. "And I don't mean the bubbles. Although they add to her allure, I'm sure."

Face morphing pink, Sarah looked from Celia to Aaron and slipped off her goggles. Aaron noticed her limp as she stepped forward. "Hi."

Celia reached for her hand. "Hi. I'm Celia. This is Amber. We've been wondering what Mina's been putting in Aaron's coffee that's put him in such a good mood lately. But now, I'm betting it's just *you* that's plunked him over the edge of joy again."

Sarah's cheeks went from pink to red.

Aaron shot Celia a stern glower.

Which she ignored. As usual. Manny put a firm hand on her arm and dragged her to the kitchen.

"I'm Amber." Joel's wife shook Sarah's hand then smiled at Aaron. "Having fun?"

"We, uh, were just—"

"Having fun. Yes," Sarah answered with confidence he envied. She pulled off the scuba flippers Aaron had loaned her.

"Nothing wrong with that," Amber said. "Pleasure to make your acquaintance."

Sarah smiled. "Nice meeting you, Amber."

He noticed Sarah's blush deepen as she stooped to help the boys. But he didn't get the feeling the flush was from embarrassment. She looked in pain.

Manny stepped close as Aaron helped Sarah off with the leaf blower. "We knocked. Several times. But you must have been too preoccupied to notice." His mouth twitched as though to laugh. But he pulled his lips in. Then he sent a sincere look to Aaron. "Like the lady said. There's nothing wrong with having fun."

He grinned at Sarah. "Nice to meet you. I'm Sergeant Peña. And this is Master Sergeant Montgomery. But you can call us Manny and Joel."

Sarah nodded and rose from setting the goggles on the hall table. Her pace slowed, proving she was in pain. Her breathing hitched and ramped faster than normal, too.

Aaron turned to Celia and Amber. "Could you guys get the boys in the upstairs tub?"

"Sure." They eyed him and Sarah with cursory looks.

Wearing a compassionate expression, Aaron stepped close. "Sarah, are you hurt?"

She bit her lip. "A little."

"What's wrong?" He waved Joel and Manny toward the kitchen.

"I pulled something lifting one of the boys earlier. It's nothing I'm sure."

Aaron eyed her carefully. "Somehow I don't buy that. Here." He led her to the living-room couch. "I'll get the ice pack."

"Uh, it's melted. In the bathroom I think. Or Cricket the goose might have run off with it." She giggled.

Aaron smiled. "Seems he has a penchant for swiping things."

She stretched out on the couch.

Aaron rose. "I'll make you another. Lie on your stomach if you are able. Can you take Motrin?"

She nodded. "If they're 200 milligrams, I'll take three."

"An adult dose is always 200 milligrams. And I'm always just a phone call away. Please remember that." Aaron stepped out, leaving an arctic chill in the room.

Something had shifted in him. He seemed displeased. Well, no wonder. The house had fallen apart in his absence. But he hadn't seemed moody until his coworkers, or whatever they were called, had shown. Was he embarrassed at their teasing? Irritated? Yes, that must have been it.

Manny and Joel talked with Aaron in the kitchen in hushed tones. The little boys splashed upstairs in the tub with the men's wives. That they'd come help Aaron in Mina's absence made her thankful he had friends like that. Even if they did tease.

Aaron could use a little humor in his life. Sarah peered over her hands at the bubble-infested hallway.

And thanked God for the blessing of Bryce and Braden's detergent mishap and the fun memory for their family that it had created here today.

"Here." Aaron came back in with a cup of water and the pain reliever. She sat up and drank it down.

"Lie on your stomach," Aaron instructed.

Then he proceeded to massage her lower back. "Point where it hurts."

She aimed a thumb at the spot, really, really glad Aaron's coworkers had just walked into the room. His hands kneading her back caused another kind of electricity to dance along her nerve endings. A very pleasant dance that she wished didn't feel so wonderful. On top of everything else, the man was a master masseur. "Right there," she said as his fingers found the knot.

"I think it's just a muscle spasm. But if it's not better by morning, you need to see a physician or a chiropractor."

"Okay." But he needed to work in the morning,

which meant she needed to work in the morning. "What about the boys?" Sarah turned her face to see him, then wished she hadn't.

The tender look in his eyes caused her heart to curl up in a contented ball. Maybe she'd imagined his displeasure earlier. He seemed fine now.

"Amber can watch them for a couple hours if need be," Joel offered.

Aaron nodded and kept working the knot out. "Better?"

Sarah nodded and averted her face. "I think I'm fine now."

"I think the knot's still there." He continued to knead.

And she continued to need him to stop. For the closeness was wreaking havoc with her senses and making her wish for a companionship that had nothing to do with an employee/employer relationship. But a meaningful, romantic relationship like those his uncommonly bonded team seemed to have with their wives.

Sarah slipped from underneath the magic of his hand. "If—if you don't mind, I think I'll cut out early. Head upstairs for a warm bath, sans bubbles, and rest." And collect her wayward thoughts.

"Sans bubbles?" He gave a hearty laugh. It reached in and wrapped its strength around her heart. Never before had a man had this much power over her emotions, will and mind.

And never before had she this much trouble holding old wishes at bay.

Wishes for a family of her own.

A family that included children to love. And a hunky man to come home to her. A helpmate to care for. The kind of man who would lovingly dole out dizzying, delightful backrubs.

A man like Aaron.

Who was so far out of her league and out of her reach, and so far beyond what she deserved after the wrong choices she'd made and the consequences of them, that she was crazy to even entertain this attraction.

Therefore she'd go to her room, pray and hope that by tomorrow, the back pain and the deeper pain of useless hoping for a nonexistent knight to carry her away would dissipate.

"I'm going to head upstairs. Thanks."

Aaron looked at her oddly. "Okay, yeah, sure." His voice didn't sound convinced.

She rose.

"Nice meeting you," Sarah called to Joel and Manny, seated at the counter barstools sipping sodas.

Joel nodded. "Likewise, Sarah."

"Later." Manny nodded at her and let a grin slip when his gaze transferred from her to Aaron and back.

"Sarah, you okay?" Aaron followed.

"I will be," she called, not stopping her trek to the stairs. The more the memory of Aaron's team members' open grins teased her mind, the more determination dogged her steps to weed out these wayward emotions.

And she'd especially pray that the silliness of this

sudden want for companionship and Aaron's affection would all *go away!*

Time to buckle down, woman up and focus on the job, the whole job and nothing but the job.

She'd been sent to this family. As their nanny. Nothing more. And she would not let herself want for more.

No matter how badly her heart longed to hope.

Her past would never let her get away with it.

Chapter Ten

"She got away with it!" Bryce exclaimed and dropped the spade in the dirt. Apparently Randy was a little girl goose with an alias named Randa who liked to peck and steal flower seeds. Sarah and Braden looked at one another and laughed.

"Daddy's home!" Braden rose, also abandoning his garden spade.

Sarah turned at the sound of Aaron's SUV coming down the driveway. The sound always infused her with a sense of elation. She looked forward more and more to his returns from the DZ.

He waved as he pulled up. His eyes brushed the boys but rested on her. Why did that stretch her grin out of control?

She led the boys to greet him as he exited his vehicle. "You and your stomach will be glad to know that Mina returned today. We picked her up from the airport."

"Hey, your cooking's not that bad." Aaron grinned

and hugged the boys, then leaned in as if to plant a kiss on her cheek. How abruptly dumb she felt when he brushed soil off her cheek instead.

He looked around the yard. "More landscaping?"

"Is that okay?"

Aaron looked at her like, *is this girl for real?* "Wow. A woman who jumps in with both bejeweled blue flip-flops."

He'd noticed her shoes? She squished her toes together.

He leaned in, eyed her feet and grinned. "I don't meet many women who wear flip-flops deep into fall."

"I don't get the feeling you meet many women at all, then."

The statement shocked them both.

Why hadn't she thought before she'd spoken?

Regret shoved her hand to rest on his arm. "I'm sorry. I know you're a widower. I hope I didn't offend you. It was a lame and insensitive joke. I overstepped my bounds."

His gaze dropped to where her hand rested on him. As if the motion surprised him. Had it made him uncomfortable? She felt frozen, not knowing whether to move her hand or leave it.

Then he lifted his face, which looked pleased indeed, and shook his head. "Not at all."

Nothing was overstepped, that is, except for the bounds of his heart that he'd worked so hard to secure after Donna died.

A sick feeling slogged to the surface, effectively cutting off any romantic ideals.

Sarah is here for the boys and only for the boys. Don't forget that.

He placed his hands on Bryce's and Braden's shoulders. "I'm proud of you guys for helping Miss Sarah."

"We love her." Bryce hunkered to shove dirt around with his spade.

Braden sat beside his brother and helped dig holes. "Yeah. Do you love Miss Sarah, Daddy?"

Sarah's head lifted sharply. Wind blew tendrils of hair across her face, but not enough to hide widening eyes or the blush creeping across her cheeks.

"I, er, I, uh, I'm really glad that she's here."

"But do you lo-ove her?"

He felt nothing but baffled. "I—"

Sarah stepped forward. "He loves that I'm here. How about we go in and get cleaned up for dinner?"

She winked at Aaron as she passed and whispered, "Distraction is a wonderful tool."

Heat coming to his ears, Aaron smiled and nodded.

Aaron descended the stairs the next morning having showered after running. Water splashes and pleasant laughter greeted him.

Sarah. And the boys. He eyed his watch. Up early.

His steps slowed as squeals, giggling and voices bounced off the bathroom walls and traveled around the corner and up the stairs.

"Whoops. Braden, wait until I get Bryce out of the

tub. Braden...Braden! Come back here." Sarah's voice rose with each word.

A streak of soppy flesh blew by Aaron. He cleared the last four steps in time to head Braden off at the pass. The child had that "about to be naughty" look.

"Stop, son. You're getting water all over the tiles. Mina could fall. Obey Miss Sarah. Now." He picked Braden up. One foot in the bathroom door, one foot out, Sarah actively watched where they stood in the hall. Out of respect, Aaron had tried to train the boys to address Mina as Miss Mina—but she had asked him not to because she wanted to seem more like family.

Braden looked as if he wanted to giggle fiendishly and cry at the same time. Squirming sideways, Braden tried to disengage from Aaron's grip. Unable, he scowled.

"Braden, don't look at me in that tone of voice." Aaron gently twisted Braden to face him.

"Okay, Dad." He made impressively loud and extensive "I'm unhappy and want the neighborhood to know it" growling noises.

Oven mittens in hand, Mina scurried out of the kitchen. "What on earth?" She looked from Aaron to Braden to Sarah, who stepped out into the hall.

Bryce could be heard obliviously singing, badly, in the bathroom. Then incessant flushing of the commode. Sarah dashed inside the bathroom. "Oh, no. Buddy. Only once. It'll overflow, remember?"

Aaron released Braden. He fled to Sarah, who held out his toothbrush.

Braden attempted to run from the toothbrush she brandished. Sarah halted him and cautioned Mina, "Wait. The floor is slick. We have a zooming human mop slopping water trails around here this morning." Sarah eyed Braden with a flare of warning in her eyes that surprised even Aaron. Must have surprised Braden, too, because he froze in place.

And Sarah scores! Arms folded now, Aaron smiled in favor of her small victory, but dipped his head so Braden couldn't see.

"I don't like you anymore!" Braden yelled. Sarah handed him his toothbrush and pointed to the bathroom like drill sergeants point to earth when they want push-ups from insubordinate boot campers.

Calmly, Sarah put a towel down and mopped up the hallway moisture. "You don't have to like me. But you do have to do what I say. However, I still like you, even when you disobey."

Braden sulked in place for a second then slogged to the sink as if every step pained him. "Fine."

"Ay, that boy!" Mina muttered to herself and went back into the kitchen, from where something sweet-smelling originated.

Sarah walked back into the bathroom where Bryce, now wrapped in a towel, was visible brushing his teeth beside Braden. Wait. Aaron, walking past, zoomed his head back around. Bryce brushing his teeth? Sure enough. A sight to behold. Especially since Bryce hated brushing more than Braden did. Aaron always encountered a battle. So most times he just gave up, figuring he'd get them in the habit later. He leaned close to Sarah, now combing Braden's hair. Miraculously, he let her without a war. "How'd you get Bryce to brush his teeth?"

"Tickets."

"Tickets?"

"It's a reward system I set in place. I'll explain later. Braden, hold still."

"He needs a haircut. They both do." He felt bad for neglecting that, too. He'd been so pressed for time.

"I see that. If it's all right with you, I'll take them next week if you tell me where."

"I usually just buzz it." Aaron stood at the bathroom door and grinned. "But you could help me."

She paused in her combing motions to eye him above Bryce's head. "Why do I get the feeling you're luring me into a devious trap?"

"Am not." But he laughed. "Okay, I will warn you that Bryce is afraid of the electric razor."

Braden scowled. "He's afraid of ev-er-y-thing. Even the vacuum and the blender."

Sarah eyed Bryce over her shoulder and bent to Braden's ear, hands sidling his head in a gentle manner. "Hey, cool it. You wouldn't want someone broadcasting things you're afraid of. Would you?"

He quieted and shook his head. "No, ma'am."

"The fearless Braden, afraid? Of what?" Aaron looked to Sarah but she averted her gaze.

So did Braden. "Nothin'." He scowled and looked down.

Sarah cast Aaron a firm, imploring "don't ask" look.

He nodded, but still wondered about Braden's fear that she'd obviously discovered and which he knew nothing about. He also wondered about the ticket mission she'd tasked the boys to. What was that all about?

"Trust me," she mouthed softly, as though perceiving his thoughts.

He nodded.

"Mighty spiffy," she said to Braden. "Now can you finish dressing for another ticket?"

"Yeah!" He shuttled to the stack of neatly pressed clothes on the vanity.

Sarah turned to Bryce, still in front of the mirror. He'd likely scrubbed his tooth enamel off by now, he brushed so vigorously. "Good job, buddy. Now where's your comb?"

Satisfied Sarah had things under control in the bathroom, Aaron joined Mina in the kitchen. "Why the child enjoys mischief so much I don't know," he said of Braden while reaching over her shoulder to snitch one of the halves of buttered toast.

Mina smacked his knuckles with her spatula. "Oh, yes, you do. Because you were, and still are, exactly like him. But you're also sensitive like Bryce. You're just better than he is at hiding it."

Aaron laughed and helped her move breakfast to the table. Sarah and the boys joined them.

Sarah looked momentarily crestfallen. "Oh, goodness. I guess it was sort of dumb of me to have them brush their teeth before breakfast." She nibbled her lip. The morning must have frazzled her more than she'd let on.

Bryce sucked in a breath. "Miss Sarah! You're not supposed to say the D word!"

"Maybe if you go to church with us, you'll know the bad words," Braden added.

The boys' words seemed to sober Sarah. Aaron knew she prayed, worshipped and otherwise maintained an intimate relationship with God. But what was her aversion to church?

Aaron reached for her hand and Mina's. "You'll get the hang of it all. It's good you're conscientious. Don't be so hard on yourself." And he meant it. "Let's pray."

The boys joined hands and bowed their heads, but Bryce peeked at Sarah while Braden's hand sneaked out for the toast.

Mina bowed her head. But snickered.

Sarah and Aaron raised their heads slightly to eye Mina.

Shoulders hunched, she laughed into a napkin pressed to her mouth. After a moment, she looked up. "I'm sorry. I mean no disrespect to the Lord, but, Aaron Michael, were it left up to you, those boys would go weeks without brushing their hair or their teeth."

Sarah smiled and dipped her head again.

Aaron felt his ears growing red. "She's right. But I'm sure Miss Sarah will intercept all the incoming missiles of tooth decay and unruly hair around here."

"I'll say Amen to that." Mina dipped her head. "Right after we pray. Aaron?"

He eyed the table, mouth drooling to polish off Mina's oatmeal, toast and thickly sliced bacon. His favorite kind.

It had been a long time since Mina had gone to this much trouble for breakfast. A sense of gratitude melted into him like the butter into Mina's Texas toast.

He hadn't seen her so relaxed in the morning in a long time. Though he always tried to help her with the typical Sunday-morning chaos, she always felt the need to help him ready the boys in addition to cooking a hot breakfast and then cleaning after.

Today she must have entrusted Sarah with some tasks because otherwise she never left the kitchen until time to sit down to eat.

Aaron bowed his head. "Lord, bless the food and the hands that prepared it." Aaron squeezed Mina's hand. Then Sarah's. "And thank You for bringing Sarah here to be with us."

The doorbell rang.

"Excuse me." Aaron wiped his mouth then rose to answer it.

He opened the door. Ashleigh, looking ten kinds of ticked, stood staccato-tapping her boot in the key of impatient on the other side. Before he could move aside, she barreled past him.

"Hey, what—?" He followed her surge toward the dining room, where voices wafted.

Mina stood. "Ash! You're back."

Sarah rose and faced Ash, who acted like she didn't see Sarah though she stood directly in front of her.

How absolutely odd.

Mina bustled around the table and hugged Ash. Ash stiffened. Not unusual. Though she was acting strange. Especially when she turned a hard gaze on Sarah.

Sarah blinked and held out her hand. "Hi—"

Ash ignored it and folded her arms in obvious hostility.

Mina watched the two with mounting concern. She eyed Aaron. He shrugged. Sarah lowered her hand, averted her gaze and, appearing to shrink with as much dignity as possible, sat down, nibbling her food.

The entire meal, increasing amounts of tension charged the air. Mostly coming from Ash and especially when Aaron engaged Sarah in conversation. Only the boys' chatter and clacking of silverware against plates pervaded.

Once she finished eating, Ash wiped her mouth and rose, then stalked around the table in a slow, vulturelike hover, never taking her eyes off Sarah. Until Ash got to the twins.

"How're my snuggle bugs?" Ash hugged both boys, then sent Sarah another lethal look.

Having had enough, Aaron wadded up his napkin and set it firmly on the table while issuing Ash a direct gaze. He jerked his head toward the guest room she normally used when she visited.

Ash rose amid the obvious tension at the table and followed.

"First off, welcome home. Second off, what was that nonsense back there?"

Ash tossed her suitcase on the bed. "Nothing."

"So total hostility resides in your eyes and tone toward Sarah for fun?"

She shot him a look meant to wither. She yanked her suitcase zipper and pulled her black house slippers from it. Wearing house shoes during the day with clothes was something she did when extremely stressed or tired—which was rare.

"Bad job overseas?" Sometimes Ash plunged into tart moods when her skip-tracing efforts didn't produce.

"Nope. We got the crook." Ash kicked off her shoes in the direction of the door where Sarah approached cautiously.

She stepped over the shoes and faced Ashleigh. "Hi. I'm Sarah Gra—"

"I know exactly who you are." Feet jammed into her slippers, Ash coolly walked off.

Aaron stared at Sarah a moment then followed Ashleigh.

"Ash, what was that all about?"

"What?"

"Don't play innocent. You were intentionally hostile toward the nanny. I don't like that you were rude to her. I think you should apologize to her and tell me what your problem is."

She tugged stuff from her overnight bag and set items on the bathroom counter. "I don't like her. And that's all I'm gonna say. For now."

The words and implications crimped Aaron's insides. Ash was on the move again. Aaron trailed after her. "Did you get my messages?"

"Yup." Back in the bedroom now, she shoved clothes in the spare dresser. He guessed she intended to stay a while. Normally she lived out of a suitcase while here.

"Did you find something?"

She turned sharply. "I said…that's all I'm going to say. For now." Her face softened a bit as she held his gaze in an uncharacteristic tenderness. "Trust me on this, okay? My reasons for not telling you are sound. So let me do my job and be your sister."

"Okay." He trusted her enough to know that if she'd found something of concern, she'd have told him upfront. Especially something dangerous. Ashleigh was ruthless in finding information, but she was just as ruthless in withholding it until she was sure her instincts were on target, unless someone's life was at stake. Otherwise she didn't gamble with revealing information. Not even to him. And he'd always respected her for that.

If she wasn't talking, she didn't have all the information she needed to come to a conclusion.

Until she talked, he'd trust that God would bring to light anything of concern.

Another possibility was maybe Ash'd picked up on the tangible attraction between him and Sarah that Aaron found himself hard-pressed to hide. Made sense. After all, the anniversary of Donna's death was dawning, and Ash had been the one to introduce him to Donna. The two women had been best friends, inseparable for years before and after Aaron had dated and married Donna. Ash had been as devastated by Donna's death as Aaron had.

Was this obvious hostility Ash harbored toward Sarah because of Donna?

Or something else?

Mina turned to Sarah as they put breakfast dishes away. "Don't mind Ashleigh. She's a temperamental little thing."

"She's not so little. I think she could take me." Sarah laughed. Then grew serious. "I can tell she doesn't like me."

"She doesn't like anyone. I'm betting she doesn't even like herself. Though I concede she does love her family. But don't worry. Aaron will stick up for you. He won't stand for her being rude to you. I guarantee he's in there defending you and giving her the third degree."

"I hate to be the one to cause problems between them."

"Ash delights in causing problems of her own accord. Trust me. I love her but, oy! She can be contentious."

"She looks so much like Aaron."

"They're twins. Their parents raised Ash and Aaron to know the Lord. They were missionaries, and died tragically in a plane crash. Ash has been bitter and cynical since."

"I wondered why there weren't more grandparents in the picture." She eyed Bryce and Braden, who were out of earshot. Sarah felt pangs of compassion for the boys. "At least they have you."

Mina smiled. "And now you."

"Thanks, Mina. I've already grown to love them."

"All three? Or just two?"

Sarah flushed. "Wha—?"

Mina splashed water at Sarah. "I'm kidding, *mija*. You're fun to tease."

"Mina, what's *mija?*"

"It's an affectionate term for 'daughter.'"

"Thank you. That means a lot."

Mina grinned. "And just between you and me, I think Ash is peeved because she's jealous."

"Of?"

"You. She loves her brother's affection for one. For another, his late wife was Ash's best friend. She's hostile toward anyone he comes in contact with."

"But I'm just the nanny."

Mina's hand covered her mouth, but the snicker slipped through. "Oh, sure. That's right. I forgot." Another snicker. "That's why he looks at you like he could devour you whole," she murmured as she went about cleaning up the kitchen.

Sarah shook her head and escaped to help the boys wash their hands.

Minutes later at the faucet, Mina pulled off her apron and set it aside. "Sure you don't want to go to church with us?"

"Another day." Sarah let the water out of the sink knowing very well she should go.

After Aaron, Mina and the boys left for church, Sarah slipped to her room to go through her mail and write letters.

Where had Ashleigh gone? Not to church.

Sarah opened a translated letter from the overseas child sponsorship program she supported. After placing the child's picture in a frame on the room's tiny roll-top desk, she settled herself into the chair to write to another child. One from long ago. After praying, she opened her eyes and, hard as it was, that raw place in her heart. She put pen to the card she'd hand-fashioned:

I hope you have a good church home and courage to attend. I pray you have people around you to bring you joy. I hope you are warm and safe. I hope you know God loves you. I pray for you every day. Signed, Sarah.

A *crunch* at her door caused her to jump. Ash. She knew it without turning around. Methodical footsteps. Aaron's twin stood above Sarah now, apple in hand, acid for eyes that burned across Sarah, then the child's picture on her desk. A scoffing sound grated out of her. "How ironic."

What did that mean?

"You can't change a cruel world. Thinking you can make a difference is ignorant and presumptuous."

"I can make a difference to her." Sarah eyed the needy child's face in the frame. Tried not to let anger take hold of her over Ashleigh's rudeness. "And better *her* world."

Another *crunch.* "There are too many starving children to help. What does it matter?"

"It matters to this one." She picked up the picture and cradled it in her hands." Then dropped her voice to a whisper. "And it matters to me."

"Not buyin' it." *Crunch. Crunch.*

Unnerving as it was, Sarah turned to meet Ashleigh's venomous gaze. "You obviously don't like me. I have no idea why. But we may as well try to get along for the family's sake."

Ashleigh's gaze narrowed. "And you obviously don't have a clue. If I have my way, we won't have a reason to get along because you won't be here. And you are *not* a part of this family."

Sarah stood. What on earth was wrong with this woman? Before Sarah could think of a worthy retort, Ash crunched hard into her apple, slammed an item on Sarah's desk, and left.

A swath of purple cloth.

Sarah stared at it. Arms numbed. Mind reeled.

"No." She couldn't know, she couldn't know, she couldn't— Fingers cold and hands trembling, Sarah lifted the cotton material and held it against her pounding heart. Clenched her eyes while images swarmed her like a horde of angry stinging wasps.

The little girl she'd struck had been wearing purple

house slippers. Sarah knew because one had gotten knocked off in the impact and landed in a muddy ditch, along with the brown backpack. Sarah had found both later.

This had to be a coincidence. Right?

But it made no sense. The purple cloth. Ashleigh's unreasonable hostility. No, it didn't make one shred of sense.

Unless Ashleigh knew about the accident.

Then it made perfect sense.

Ashleigh's words came back to burn a path along her brain.

I know exactly who you are...

If I have my way...

Did Ashleigh *know?*

Either way, Ash was out to get rid of her.

And if Ash knew about the accident, that might be ammunition enough to cost her a job she knew she was meant for. But it was more than a job now. She'd lose her relationship with the family she'd grown to care so much about in so little time.

Especially the boys. And she just couldn't.

She put her forehead to the desk. "I know You've forgiven me. Heal Ash from whatever has made her so bitter and cynical. Work this out before Ash works me out. Amen."

Chapter Eleven

"I have never seen so many in one place," Aaron said after entering Sarah's room days later.

She eyed the monster stack of envelopes. "I found them on sale."

"I wouldn't use that many in a lifetime."

Sarah stuffed a card for her parents' anniversary inside the envelope she held. "I'll use them in a matter of months."

She'd just sealed one, in fact. She eyed the desk on which the letter—one she had yet to mail—sat. One of hundreds sent to the person who never answered.

Whether unable or unwilling, Sarah didn't know.

And that haunted her day and night.

To the point she refused to stop writing until her heart had answers. What had become of the little girl in the flowing dress?

She knew the child had survived; otherwise she'd have been charged with murder or manslaughter.

Through attorneys, she had obtained permission from the girl's parents to send letters. Though she'd written them since shortly after the accident, she hadn't mailed them for the first couple of years.

Had the child suffered a setback that didn't allow her to write? How badly had she been injured? Sarah knew from her attorney that the little girl had undergone several surgeries.

All caused by Sarah.

Though she'd chained herself to the hospital waiting room to pray for the little girl the night of the wreck, it didn't excuse her actions or excise the debilitating guilt that had made Sarah wish she'd been the one hurt instead.

She looked around for the backpack.

And found it safely on the bed.

A sound at her door made her remember Aaron was still standing there.

She swallowed with difficulty and blinked to dam a sudden rush of tears. Aaron grew quiet midsentence, so he must have noticed.

What had he even been saying?

She closed the flaps on the card-making supply box.

"So, you like crafty items?" Aaron moved close, watching her carefully. Another question shone in his eyes.

"Yes. They serve a purpose."

"Maybe you can tell me about it sometime."

She weighed her answer carefully. "Maybe I could. Maybe on the way to church one Sunday."

He gave her a kind smile. "I'd like that. In the meantime, would you like to help Mina and I plan the boys' birthday party next month?"

"Yes! Can I make the invitations? The boys can help. I have baby-green and yellow gingham cardstock."

Aaron blinked. "Gingham. Hmm."

"Or there's also this." She reached in her cardstock file and pulled out blue camouflage pages.

Aaron grinned. "Now you're talkin'."

"What else can I do to help?"

"Mind picking up supplies and groceries for the party? Mina tires easily and hates to shop."

"Sure. Not only that, I'll take over the regular family grocery shopping. I see you all keep a running list on the fridge."

He nodded. "Thanks, Sarah. Even though I saw that you added cereal straws to that list." He leaned back and folded his arms across his chest, but never ceased smiling.

She sat straighter and grinned. "Guilty. And they don't have that much sugar in them. Hey, wait. How did you know my handwriting?"

"I notice everything about you, Sarah."

Gulp. "Everything?"

He rose, tousling her hair as he did so. "Yep. Everything."

He frequently tousled the boys' hair, yet at the end of the tousle of her hair, Aaron's fingers softened into more of a caress. And the ministration of his fingers became more of a massage. And there was nothing daddyish about it.

Nor was the tender look flaring in his eyes bossish.

About to melt into her chair, Sarah leaned into his hand. "Aaron—"

Though he looked as if he wanted to reach for her, his arms loosened then fell to his side instead.

"Aaron, I— We—"

He shook his head and put a finger to her mouth in what was definitely an intimate rather than silencing gesture. "Let's not."

He didn't have to finish for her to know. He meant "let's not talk about it yet." Though his words had cut hers short, hope grew alive in his unmistakably interested eyes. Also residing in their warm blue depths was the invitation to let what was happening between them emotionally lead where it may.

"Where are you leading me?" Sarah stuck her hand over her eyes as instructed by Braden upon exiting the car three weeks later. She'd just arrived back from picking up groceries when Braden rushed her and ordered her to cover her eyes.

Bryce giggled. "A surprise! No peeking!"

"Oh! Whatever could it be?" She peeked enough to get herself and the grocery sack inside without tripping and spilling its contents.

"C'm'ere Miss Sarah!" Bryce tugged her around the corner of the kitchen. "But keep your eyes closed."

"Okay."

"Don't peek!" Braden admonished.

"I won't." Sarah's hate-to-be-bored brain shifted into ponder gear while she waited for the boys to unveil whatever it was she was standing here, hand over closed eyes, waiting for.

She and the boys had settled into a nice routine and Mina had been able to make another trip to New Mexico to visit her mom.

Aaron had been talking to Sarah more and more about things other than the boys. They'd developed a friendly rapport that Sarah felt bad was semi-one-sided, in that he'd shown interest in her life outside of the Petrowski crew, yet there wasn't much she could share without fear of unearthing a past she'd rather stay buried.

Aaron continued to offer gentle invitations to church. She'd offered polite refusals. Yet she sensed that before long he'd hold her accountable for her lack of plugging in with a body of believers. And he had every right to.

After all, she'd painted herself to be someone who would influence his sons toward a healthy relationship with God. Something she knew herself was difficult to maintain without a strong commitment to a healthy church home.

Give me courage to be involved in social situations without fear of running into people like Officer Stallings.

She'd rather be outside and around people. But paralyzing fear of someone recognizing her kept her reclusive.

"Daddy hanged it." Braden lifted his chest and poked his finger at the week's drawings on the fridge.

Sarah smiled as she brushed fingers over the carefully crayoned artwork that the boys had put alongside the others they'd drawn Aaron since her first visits.

This was the big surprise? "I'm glad he loved the pictures you made."

Bryce poked another paper at her. "I made this one for just for you."

Braden jumped ahead of Bryce. "Yeah! And I helped him."

"Aww. I love it! You're such good artists."

Braden scowled and poked the paper. "You got it upside down."

Whoops. "Oh. Well, of course. I knew that. I just wanted to view it from all angles. It's such a masterpiece."

That seemed to appease.

"And…we made this one for you, too. It's the surprise." Braden bumped his shoulder into Bryce and they erupted into giggles.

"Well, isn't this cozy." Ash brushed by them, bumping Sarah's shoulder hard with her arm. Had the boys not been there, Sarah might have yanked Ash by her ponytail. Of course Ash would have stomped her, but the initial pleasure of catching Ash off guard might have been worth it.

Lord, forgive me for entertaining fantasies of violence.

Sarah leaned close enough to Ash that the boys couldn't hear. "I got the gift you left on my dresser. Please stay out of my room when I'm not in there." Sarah meant the lavender lace ribbon Ash had to have left on her desk. The eerie likeness of Ash's "gifts" to items from the accident scene with the little girl unnerved Sarah. Macy had been wearing purple lace in her pigtails. The EMTs had taken them off to assess Macy's skull for fractures. Sarah had rescued the ribbon, unable to leave it in the bloody mud where it would be buried. A colossal reminder and fossil of her foolishness.

"Au contraire, you were in there," Ash said, then bent to kiss the boys' foreheads. With a flip of her chin toward Sarah she was out of there.

Ash snuck into her room while she was sleeping?

Anger rose. She shoved it down and diverted her attention back to the boys' stick figures on the page. Sarah genuinely interested herself in the pictures. And noticed an honestly discernable image on the paper. Joy and pleasure filled her over the time and effort boys' put into the work.

"Boys, this is nice." She really was impressed. She could actually, sort of, in a roundabout way, make out who each of the six people were.

Bryce grinned. "It's us. Our family."

"I gathered that. This is really good, guys. Thank you."

"But, Miss Sarah, do you see the flowers in your hand?" Bryce pointed to a blotchy spot of colors.

She eyed the stick-figure woman holding the hand

of the stick-figure man in the maroon beret. She was the only stick figure brandishing anything resembling flowers.

"Um, I think so. But I thought that was Aunt Ashleigh." Especially since the stick figure was holding the hand of the stick-figure father.

"No, it's you. That's Auntie Ash back in the back of the church."

Sarah laughed at Ash's figure's trench coat, scowl and dark glasses. They certainly had her pegged.

"This room with all the chairs is your church?"

"Yeah. And you and Daddy got married in the picture."

Gulp.

"Oh. Well, um. Thanks." She knelt. "But, boys, you understand that I'm just your nanny. Right?" How it pained her to say. Pained her even more the disappointment drooping the twin sets of eyes that went straight to her heart.

"Yeah. We know. But we was just wishin' and playin' and all." Tough Braden shrugged as if he was brave. But his voice held the same fragile wistfulness as the fear he'd confided in her the day of the storm.

Fear that Sarah would one day leave as their mom had.

"But even though I'm your nanny, I don't plan to go away. Okay?"

An uncharacteristic vulnerability glistened in Braden's eyes. "Okay." He reached and hugged her. She set the picture on the counter.

"You wa white Myth There-a. Daddy wubbed the dwa-ingths."

What on earth was wrong with his speech?

She bent. "Bryce…what's in your mouth?"

His eyes grew wide and his mouth grew tight.

"Open it, please. Now."

A juicy Lego appeared.

She washed it beneath warm water and rubbed disinfecting soap over it. "You shouldn't put things like that in your mouth." She rinsed off the soap.

Bryce's head bent and his face crumpled.

She knelt and hugged Bryce. "I'm not mad at you. Just concerned about your safety."

"Okay." He hugged her neck tightly.

The three retreated to the couch for more drawing and story time.

Once seated, Bryce crawled partway in her lap and took gentle hold of strands of her hair, which she'd left down today.

"Miss Sarah?"

"Yeah?"

"Can I give you a butterfly kiss?"

"What's that?"

Bryce leaned in and blinked his eyelashes on her cheek.

"It tickles." She giggled.

"It means I love you."

"Ahh. Well, I love you, too."

"Then can I have butterfly kisses?"

She leaned in and blinked on his cheek until he giggled and hugged her.

Braden watched them with a funny expression. "Butterfly kisses are dumb."

"Is that right?" Sarah tried not to laugh because for once Bryce scowled at Braden. Should she point out the D-word infraction? Nah, she'd let it slide this time.

"Eskimo kisses are better." Braden went back to drawing.

Bryce sighed. "Miss Sarah? You know what is an Eskimo kiss?"

"I think so." She leaned forward and brushed her nose against Bryce's.

He giggled and grabbed his nose and rubbed his eyes. "That makes me see funny."

"I notice you went cross-eyed." She chuckled.

"See, that's why butterfly kisses are better," he said.

"Eskimo," Braden said, still seated at the coffee table, coloring on sheets of paper.

"Butterfly."

"Eskimo!"

"Butterfly!"

"Boys."

"Sorry." Bryce leaned against her shoulder.

Holding the snuggle bug of the two, Sarah leaned forward. "Whatcha drawing?" she asked Braden.

"An airplane. My daddy jumps out of them when they're high in the air." He made zooming sounds and "flew" a hand above his head.

Sarah tucked her stocking-clad feet beneath her on the couch. "He must be brave."

"He is." Bryce shifted. "I'm scared of stuff but Braden's not scared of anything."

"Yes, I am. Miss Sarah?" Braden said. "I'm scared you'll hafta go away like Mommy did."

"I know. But I don't think I will, okay?"

Not unless Ash had her way.

Sarah brushed a hand along Braden's forehead. "Do you remember your mom?" Not possible, right?

"Sometimes I dream about her. But when I'm up, I can't remember."

Bryce blinked. "Me neither. I wish I did."

"Me, too," Braden said. "We hafta look at her picture and hear Daddy and Mina and Auntie Ashleigh tell stories to know her."

Profound sadness hit Sarah on their behalf. Something in her softened a notch toward Ash. She did fiercely love the boys.

"Daddy isn't a very good mommy sometimes," Bryce sighed in dramatic tones.

Sarah tilted her head. "He's not?"

"No." Bryce leaned in and put his hands around her ear, then spoke in a loud whisper. "He makes a *terrible* omelet. Terrible."

Sarah laughed. "Well, at least he tries."

Braden sustained a look of undiluted disgust. "We wish he wouldn't."

"Good mommies know how to make the best omelets," Bryce said.

"Yeah." Braden nodded.

"Miss Sarah, will you try?"

"Try what, Bryce?"

He ran tiny hands down her cheeks. "Try to make the best omelets?" The beseeching look in Bryce's eyes said more than she imagined Bryce was even cognizant of. What if he was, even subconsciously, asking her to try to break through the barrier and be their mother?

Was it even possible their hearts knew what they'd been missing?

She swallowed. "I'll try, Bryce. For you guys, I'll try my best."

"Daddy likes cheese in his omelet. Just in case you need to know that," he whispered in a small, serious voice. Intertwined threads of hope and loss and pain and longing ran through it.

Loss he couldn't possibly remember.

"Okay. Thanks, buddy. I'll remember."

Braden sped off to the playroom.

"I'm hungry," Bryce said. "Can I have a cheese stick?"

"Sure." She rose, still holding him.

"Miss Sarah?" Bryce continued to play with her hair.

"Hmm?" She set him down but knelt to see in his eyes.

"You're aa-maaazing."

"Amazing she is."

Aaron.

Sarah froze. Tried to act unaffected by his presence.

How much had he heard?

Rising, she handed a cheese stick to Bryce and ushered him to his booster seat at the nearby island counter. But instead of going for the cheese, Bryce ran for his dad instead. Aaron scooped him up. "Hey, buddy. Did you have a good day?"

"Yes. But I missed you."

"I missed you, too."

They hugged, then Aaron placed Bryce in the booster.

"Daddy, why do you hafta work now?"

"I just do. At least for a little while. Did you enjoy Miss Sarah today?"

"Yeah! She's fun."

"I'll bet," Aaron said then moved close behind her. Heat must waft off the man at boiling point.

She turned and smiled, trying not to be nervous at his nearness. Or his inquisitive, penetrating gaze.

Had he heard the omelet exchange?

"Daddy!" Braden dropped his toy and dashed forward now that Aaron was in full view of the playroom.

He picked up Braden.

"Lookie!" Braden pointed to the refrigerator. "I made it just for you!" He aimed a finger at the picture he and Bryce had given to Sarah earlier.

Wait. Sarah thought he said he'd made it just for her.

Oh, well. So much for that. She laughed.

Until she recalled the marriage picture the boys had drawn! She snatched it off the counter and shoved it behind her back.

Aaron sent a curious glance her way before smiling at the fridge drawings. After studying it a moment, he winked at Sarah. "To an untrained eye, this would look like frizzy green hair on a blue Crayola cyclone."

"But any art expert knows it for the masterpiece that it is," she countered.

Aaron scratched a spot on his tanned forehead. Looked to her as if he'd gotten his hair buzzed closer.

Speaking of closer, he leaned in. Warm breath fanned her ear. "Remind me what exactly it is? I'm in hot water here otherwise."

"A fishing boat and birds and the moon."

"Moon in the daytime, huh?"

Sarah grinned at him, then at Bryce and Braden. "Ah, yes. Crayons can make the moon shine anywhere, any time."

"Miss Sarah, do you like my daddy?" Bryce asked.

Ack! He did *not* just ask that.

Could the floor go ahead and swallow her up now?

"Well, of course I like him. He's my boss."

"Daddy, you're not supposed to be bossy."

Aaron looked about to wilt and snicker at the same time.

The landline phone rang. Thank goodness. What an uncomfortable situation.

"Chief Petrowski," Aaron answered.

"Not hardly," Sarah, stepping away, mumbled beneath her breath. "More like *Major Distraction*."

"Boys, go play for a bit. Miss Sarah and I need to talk," he said after ending his call.

"Miss Sarah, my daddy thinks you're pretty."

She felt the color leave her face. Only to be replaced by a serious blast of heat.

A strangled cough came out of Aaron. He cast an embarrassed, apologetic glance at her.

Sarah's face blanched then flushed. He'd never seen a person's face turn that many colors at once.

"Braden, go. Play."

A scowl drew his face up. "Hmph. No fair. We wanna play with Miss Sarah, too."

Aaron coughed again. "We're not going to play. We're going to talk. Then you can play with Miss Sarah."

The boys retreated to the playroom, off the side of the dining area. He could still see them from where he stood.

Aaron motioned for Sarah to sit, then turned a barstool around and straddled it. "So, how're you doin? How are things going with the boys and the geese and the bubbles?"

She grabbed a bell pepper to chop. "Well, the boys are great. The geese seem subdued for now. And no bubbles in sight."

Aaron laughed. "Mina tells me you hardly take breaks. You know you don't have to help with housework, right?"

"I know. And I won't let helping Mina come before taking care of the boys. But I enjoy helping her when I can."

He shifted to rest his elbow on the counter. "So tell me about this ticket thing."

She pulled out a red roll of carnival-like tickets.

"They earn a ticket every time they obey or do something nice. I also revoke tickets for bad behavior after a warning. Up to nine tickets, I can take tickets away. But on the tenth ticket, I trade it in for a dollar."

"Seems to be working. They're delving into chores and working harder at getting along. They've even asked me and Mina for tickets when you weren't here."

"It's a good system. I need to get a container for their tickets."

He rested his chin on his knuckles. "How about some kind of see-through plastic jar? That way they could view how many tickets and dollars they have."

"Ooh, I like that."

And he liked how her face lit up when she said that. And how her lips moved as her tongue lingered on the *L* in the middle of the sentence. A flash of heat hit Aaron under the collar. Employee-employer. Employee-employer. Employee-employer!

What were they talking about? Oh, tickets. Right. He straightened. "Any questions?"

"Yes, did you know Bryce might grow up to be the next Superman?"

Aaron pushed up his sleeves and smiled. "He pulled a few jump maneuvers, eh?"

"Yes. He's like a human afterburner. He likes to slide down the banister with a cape flying behind him."

"I'll have a talk with him. And for what it's worth, if time-out doesn't work for Bryce, threaten to take away his cartoon time. That'll get him every time."

"Thanks. I appreciate the pointers."

"I'm not perfect, believe me. I'm still trying to figure them out myself. Not as if they came with instructions."

She laughed. "I know you've had Mina to help, but you've also done well with them on your own, Aaron." She stood. "Looks as if a heated exchange is broiling in the playroom over a robot. I'll go check it out."

"Oh, and Sarah? Before you go. There's one more thing."

"Yes?"

"I like mushrooms in my omelet, too." He grinned.

Her face flamed and she blinked, probably waiting for further explanation. Which he could not provide because he could not explain from where the boldness came to say it. He'd meant it as a defusing joke. But now that the proverbial can was open, what were they supposed to do with the worms?

Bryce approached. "We want to play Hokey Pokey."

"Okay." Sarah looked relieved at the interruption.

"Wait. We don't want anybody to feel left out." He jumped up and raced from the room. Moments later, he was tugging a confused-looking Mina into the room.

"Daddy, we want you to dance with us, too," Bryce begged.

Now Sarah was the one snickering. He'd poked fun at her over the Hokey Pokey dance.

His time of reckoning had come.

He decided to suck it up rather than cave to reluctance over how goofy he'd look. The boys dragged him into the living room, where Sarah pushed the footstool and coffee table against the wall. Mina turned on the song.

And the five of them danced.

Or tried to. Aaron couldn't get the hang of the motions until the third try. He kept falling behind because of his frequent scoping out of the front window to be sure one of his guys wasn't gonna embarrass him again by pulling up and seeing this. But Aaron soon surrendered to the fun in the song.

By this point his sons were melting with giggles and Sarah had a look of jubilant victory.

Ridiculous as it felt, he laughed as if he hadn't in ages.

The front door opened. Ashleigh breezed through the room in her typical trench coat, curly up-do and oversize sunglasses. She paused at the door. Lowered her glasses halfway. Scowled. "You've all lost it." Shaking her head, she moved on.

At least she hadn't scalded Sarah with a boiling look this time. Hopefully whatever raged in Ash's heart toward Sarah had settled down. It helped that Aaron had stuck up for Sarah.

With everyone now breathing hard and near sweaty, Mina turned down the volume. "Okay, I need to get dinner going. Or all of us will go hungry this evening."

Sarah knelt as Mina exited the room. "Boys, let's pick up the toys in there and wash up for dinner."

After helping Sarah oversee the toy pickup, Aaron joined Mina in the kitchen.

"Aaron, I have not seen you laugh and joke and play like that in years." Mina pulled items from the fridge.

"I know. What was up with that?" He shook his head and laughed.

"It was your sense of humor awakening." Mina opened a drawer and tugged out a chopping board.

He thought about what she said. When *was* the last time he'd laughed like that? He eyed Sarah interacting with his children. "She's contagious."

"Yes. Sarah has a way of bringing out the fun in people."

"She said even Ash didn't verbally incinerate her this week."

Mina chuckled. "Could be because Sarah stood up for herself every time Ash spewed snide remarks. It helps that you defend Sarah at every turn, too."

"I wonder what the deal is with those two?"

"I'm betting Ash is struggling to see another young woman in the house. An attractive young woman." She sent Aaron a testing look. "I haven't gallivanted around like a little kid in a long time. It made years melt off me and I almost felt like a carefree child again without the worries of this world."

"I'm glad, Mina. Also glad you didn't wear yourself out."

"She'll be good for this family, Aaron. Good for all of us." She pulled out a bag of potatoes. Washed and peeled them. "Even Ash, once she gets over whatever's making her crotchety."

"I'm glad to hear you say that. Maybe Sarah can

be for my children what you were for me and Ash growing up."

Tears sparkled in her eyes. "Now don't go telling her that I was you and Ashleigh Kate's nanny growing up or she'll think I'm as old as I am."

Aaron laughed and reached for a piece of raw tater, something he'd always done as a kid, which drove Mina nuts.

"Still stealin' my taters before I can cook 'em. Some things never change." Mina knocked his knuckle with a potato peeler.

"Ouch." Rubbing his knuckles, Aaron laughed. "Right. Some things never change." He had many knuckle scars to prove it.

"But some things do." A glint of knowing entered her eyes. "And I have a feeling, Aaron Michael," she said, looking at Sarah through the semi-open door, "that things are about to change in ways you never imagined."

Chapter Twelve

What a difference!

Laughter met Sarah as she cracked her bedroom window Saturday morning. She drank in the delight on Aaron's face as he watched Bryce chase Braden across the yard. It was her day off, yet all she wanted was to go play with the boys. She'd write her letter later. Tugging on her jogging shoes and jacket, she scrambled downstairs. "Can I join?"

Aaron turned at her voice. Their gazes locked. His steps slowed to a near stop. Torso angled toward her, he tilted his head and flashed a smile that could compete with the sun.

After playing a few rounds of catch, the boys grew bored, so Aaron threw Sarah the ball instead.

After a few back-and-forth tosses, Aaron stepped backward and tossed her a curveball. She tilted her glove, slid and caught it.

Aaron grinned. "Wow. Let's see what else you got."

He threw her two fastballs, which she also caught. He pulled his bottom lip over his top one, jutted his chin and bobbed his head in long, slow nods. "Impressive. You're a great catch, Sarah." His gaze lingered. She realized the double meaning. Her face flamed. His grin widened. An awkward but exhilarating moment passed. He didn't apologize or correct or even explain his statement, which left her no clue as to whether he meant it exactly the way his words expressed it, or the way the glow of interest in his eyes suggested it. His words were intentional.

Moments later Ashleigh's black Hummer rumbled down the driveway. The twins rushed over. Aaron, clear across the yard, called out a warning to slow down. Braden either didn't hear or he ignored because he sped ahead. The Hummer was so tall. Did Ash even see the boys? The world suddenly bogged to slow motion and Sarah's knees weakened. *Braden, stop. Please stop!*

But he didn't, and neither did Ash. And they looked to be on a collision course. Sarah knew the fragile child would be no match for a two-ton Hummer. Aaron sprinted toward Braden. Time stood still. Ash kept coming.

"Look out!" Nausea hit her at the thought of Braden getting hit. Old memories bobbed to the surface, siphoning strength from Sarah's knees, making it hard to run. So she screamed with everything she had.

Just in time, Aaron grabbed Braden and Ash braked.

Heaving, Sarah slumped to the ground, trembling and feeling faint. Aaron, looking severely concerned, set Braden down and started toward her, only to be distracted by a streak of movement to his left. Braden dashed forward down the long driveway.

"Son! Slow down."

Too late. Braden tripped on one of the landscape bricks. Sarah watched, helpless, as he flew face-first toward the asphalt.

Aaron surged forward like a lightning bolt, catching him before his face hit.

Rising, Sarah let out the breath she'd sucked in and slung the glove aside. Ash flung the car door open and raced Sarah to the spot.

Braden's cries pierced her heart. She knelt where his dad hovered over him.

Ash bent. "Oh, no."

Fear of spewing prevented Sarah from speaking. Ash turned to her then, taking in her Richter-worthy trembling. Sarah averted her gaze and drew deep breaths so she could talk again.

"Is he all right?" Words wobbled. She leaned in.

Aaron held Braden's scraped-raw hands in his own and tilted them to inspect. "Yeah. He's tough. He'll be all right. Won't ya, bud?"

Braden's quivering bottom lip stuck out and tears wavered on his lashes. But he nodded his head nonetheless.

It amazed her how Aaron remained calm, yet she could tell he felt bad that Braden bit the dust. Ash eyed

Braden and picked up Bryce. She actually looked compassionate for once, until she caught Sarah studying her. She narrowed her gaze and headed inside the house with Bryce in arms.

Seeing Braden's bleeding palms, Sarah slid her backpack string and pulled it open. She pulled out a small first-aid kit. She extended it to Aaron, who looked peculiarly at it, then at her.

"My daddy's kit is bigger." Braden sniffed.

"But this one will do." Aaron smiled into Braden's face as he pulled a moist cleansing cloth out of the tiny kit.

"My daddy helps sick people all the time. Especially pilots whose airplanes fall down. Daddy goes and finds them. Then after he makes them all better, he rescues them from the enemy. Then he helps them some more."

She recalled Aaron's maroon beret on the mantel, right beside his wedding photo. She knew PJs were military skydiving paramedics. "Is that right? Well, your daddy sounds very brave."

Raised to be patriotic, Sarah sent Aaron an appreciative glance.

"He is." Braden sniffed again as Aaron dabbed the scrapes.

"So are you, Braden. You took a pretty hard fall there." Though it would have been unimaginably worse had Ash not stopped and Aaron not moved like lightning. She'd never seen a human move that fast and that smoothly. Adorna had mentioned he was career military. High up. And forty. While silver slivers did decorate the sides of his hair above his ears, it added the appeal of earned wisdom and attractive distinction.

The rest of the exquisitely sculpted man seemed fitter than most twenty-year-olds she knew. Today he was dressed casually in a sky-blue polo and khaki shorts and loafers. The stark blue of his wise eyes matched the limitless sky he loved to fly in.

Strong hands and long fingers ministered care to the tender skin of one of the little boys he loved more than life. His hands were a mixture of hard-earned calluses and meticulously manicured nails. And was that a different scent of aftershave than he normally wore? Not that she'd noticed.

Okay, so, yeah. Admittedly there was nothing about the man that she didn't notice. Such as how he stared at her now.

"I'm impressed that you carry a first-aid kit."

"Yep. Always prepared."

"And I finally got to see what else is in that bottomless backpack purse besides coloring books and crayons."

She laughed, but not as passionately as usual. Of course his felt subdued, too. Even though the angle she sat at cast her face in profile as she sat beside him, he'd grown too physically aware of her examination of him.

The way she looked at him when she thought he couldn't see closed the age gap between them. She had no idea how spectacular his peripheral vision was. And she had no idea how spectacular a vision she was dressed in those hip-hugging jeans and a pinkish-red shape-outlining sweater. Not at all like the sloppy, humongous Army tent she'd bummed around in the night he'd returned her phone.

For the first time in a long time he felt young enough to be attractive again. And for the first time in a long time he had a noteworthy fight on his hands: battling the impulse to pull her into his arms. Especially with remembrance of the terror embedded in that scream.

Terror that had nothing to do with today.

Yet tugging him from the other end was the logic and concern, regarding her overreaction to Ash coming down the driveway and the boys running toward the vehicle. Ash was alert and knew to be slow and careful. And Aaron had caught Braden. Would Sarah react to every near emergency like this? She'd almost lost the ability to think straight or even function. Her motor skills tanked.

Would this be a problem?

Lead me to the truth. Help her open up to me.

Aaron studied her, convinced she could handle herself physically and cognitively in any true disaster or medical emergency. He didn't get the idea she caved to fear. So the bigger question was, why had a benign situation blown up in her mind? He decided to dip his toe in turbulent waters.

"Once you calm down enough to walk, you might want to roll your windows up. Looks as if it might rain."

She looked at him sharply. "Thanks. I will. And for what it's worth, I don't normally fall apart like that."

He nodded. "I didn't figure. So why did you?"

She swallowed. "I saw a child get hit once."

He didn't know what to say. He reached a hand down.

She took it, rose on shaky legs and walked toward her car. Her tremors returned. Which left him to wonder if the accident had left the child okay.

Because Sarah certainly wasn't.

She'd obviously witnessed a trauma. Now he felt bad for saying anything.

He turned to Braden who, obviously feeling better and growing antsy, scrambled to his feet. "Son, go on inside." As he did, Aaron met Sarah at the car.

The entire backseat was full of boxes of envelopes and stationery. Looked as if she'd had more things shipped to her. He also caught sight of post office change-of-address forms.

Obvious proof she intended to stay in the area, which conflicted with Ash's pessimistic prediction that Sarah wouldn't stick around long enough to fulfill her contract. Aaron trusted Ash, yet he trusted Mina, too. And for once the women's opinions of a person didn't align.

So, which of their radars were jammed this time?

"Need help getting this stuff inside?" Aaron asked Sarah.

Still not meeting his gaze, she nodded.

He moved some kind of athletic shoe; it looked somewhere between a sandal and a sneaker.

He eyed his watch. He had a half hour to talk to Sarah before he needed to leave.

Then again, maybe not. For once, Sarah didn't look up to talking. Box in arms, she walked a silent path to the house. He followed.

Near the door she paused, taking in the yard. "If it's all right with you, I'd like to plant more things. The boys have been helping me with minor landscaping, and it'll be too cold to play outside soon."

Aaron nodded. "Yeah."

Her gaze went from the yard to the garage, then back to Aaron. "And Mina mentioned you'd like the garage cleaned out. If you want, I can go through that stuff if you'll tell me what all you want to keep."

Aaron didn't experience the grief reaction he'd expected. Relief is what he felt. "I'd love that. On both counts. In return, I'd really love to hear what trauma from your past was triggered by the near-miss with Braden and Ash's Hummer."

Sarah's movements faltered. She looked down quickly, then back up. "Deal. But in my time."

"Deal." At least she hadn't denied having a flash-back. He knew the look from commanding his combat soldiers.

Aaron fell into step beside her as they continued toward the house. Once inside, they bookended each boy by sitting on either side of Bryce and Braden on the large couch.

Bryce looked dreamily into her face. "Miss Sarah, you're pretty."

"Well, thank you, Bryce."

"Will you marry me?"

She emitted something between a gurgle and a giggle. "If we were closer in age, I'd seriously think about it. But I'm sure you'll find a wife your age when you get to be a grown-up."

"Well, my daddy is a grown-up. Will you marry him?"

Sarah swallowed. Aaron averted his gaze. The tension of embarrassment tightened around them.

"Well, I'm just your nanny."

Aaron peered at her. *Just* the nanny? Is that how she saw herself? For that matter, is that how he saw her?

No. Not by a long shot. At least not anymore.

Maybe his microscopically perceptive sister had picked up on those vibes. And maybe that was where her anti-Sarah hostility originated from.

Braden stopped coloring and perked up. "But why can't you marry the nanny, Daddy?"

"Well, son, people should love each other to be married."

Braden's eyebrows squished. "Don't you love Miss Sarah? I do."

"Me, too," Bryce added.

"Miss Sarah is a lot younger than me, boys. I'm sure she will find a husband who is her age."

Sarah brushed bangs out of her widening eyes and swallowed, clearly growing as uncomfortable in the playground of this conversation as he was and looking for the same slide out of it.

"But she's a grown-up and you're a grown-up," Braden said.

"Yeah," Bryce added.

Sarah shifted nervously on the couch, looking as if she had no idea what to say.

"Right. But there are different kinds of love. Miss Sarah works for me."

"So fire her and ask her to marry you," Braden offered.

Sarah laughed, then covered her mouth.

Aaron chuckled. "If life could only be that simple, son. Besides, she's fifteen years younger than me." He rose. "You boys tell Miss Sarah bye. She has somewhere to be."

It was Saturday.

He walked Sarah to the foyer. She'd grown unusually quiet. He held open the door. Night sounds greeted them. She stepped slowly, almost robotically toward the dusky yard. On the first step, she paused, tilting her face over her shoulder to catch his gaze. "It's only ten years, two months and twelve days."

"Excuse me?" Aaron stepped closer. She'd whispered. He wasn't sure he'd heard right, nor knew what it meant.

She raised her chin. "I'm only ten years, two months and twelve days younger." Her voice held an unmistakable earthy quality. The vulnerability in her eyes froze him on the spot.

She continued on to the car. Her words rang in his

mind. As did the question of why she'd felt it so important to point his misconception out.

After Aaron could move again, he returned to the couch, only then realizing Sarah had left her scruffy backpack. Strange. He rarely saw her without it. As if it had become a permanent Sarah appendage in his mind. Good. Gave him an excuse to call her. Fact was, he'd been looking for any excuse lately to talk to her. Be with her. Spend time together with the boys or without. Crazy. She made him feel good. He dialed her cell.

"Hello?"

"Sarah?"

"Yeah?" Her voice sounded softer than usual. Tentative. As if maybe she was embarrassed or fearful after revealing what she had before leaving.

"Two things. First, I wanted to let you know your backpack's here."

"I left it?"

"Yeah. I'll put it out of the boys' reach. Okay if I lay it on your bed?"

"Sure. What was the other thing?"

She sounded anxious. Anticipatory? Or dread-driven? He couldn't tell. He could tell she was still driving, but he knew she used a Bluetooth earpiece. He drew the world's longest breath and prayed he had guts to say what he felt.

"The other thing was something I wanted to tell you before you left." Tell her? Kiss her silly was what he'd wanted.

"Yeah?" Vulnerability resounded. She'd shared her heart and care for him and waited a return verdict.

This he could give. Yet she had no reason to fear.

That was, if she wanted this as much as he did.

"Since we're clearing things up, I wanted to let you know that you're much more than just a nanny."

A small squeak came over the phone. He might have mistaken it for strange cell interference, except that he'd heard her make that same sound the first day she'd visited the house and had become enamored of it and the boys. It was a sound he knew meant she'd drawn innocent pleasure, sweet surprise and tremendous joy from something.

That she would direct that affection toward him caused his grin to go all goofy. He shifted, holding the phone much more carefully and wishing he could hold her instead, and say these things in person so he could see her face light up the way it did when she was happy about something.

He could certainly relate. "Sarah?"

"I'm here." Definite smile in her voice.

"I just wanted you to know."

"Okay."

"I'll see you later, okay?"

"Okay. Bye, Aaron." Though the words were softly whispered, they held a promise and an awed sort of wonder that caused his pulse to loop-the-loop. He couldn't even explain whether it was a promise from him to her or a promise from her to him. Or better yet, a subliminal promise from God that there was hope for their future. Together.

After reluctantly hanging up, Aaron sat, intending to color with his sons. "You boys gonna share with Daddy?"

Bryce blinked at him. "You're coloring with us?"

"Sure? Why not? Miss Sarah does."

Much to his chagrin, Braden ripped a page out with a princess on it and handed it to Aaron, along with a pink crayon.

He wanted to laugh. If the guys could only see him now.

"Daddy, her eyes are so sparkly when she smiles."

"The princess?"

"Miss Sarah, silly."

Bryce was obviously taken with Sarah.

Aaron could relate.

"Daddy, I love Miss Sarah and I wish she would love me, too." Bryce fiddled with Aaron's sleeve.

"She does love you, son."

"I *mean,* I wish she loved us like a mommy."

"I wish she *was* our mommy," Braden added.

What could he say to that? How would they even have a concept of what a mom was? He'd talked to them about their mom, but only when they asked, which wasn't often.

"How do you boys know so much about mommies?"

"The kids at church have 'em," Braden said.

"They do, huh?"

Braden nodded. "Yeah. And daddies."

"All of them?"

"Most of them."

"We wish we had a mommy, too." Bryce's voice dialed down.

Aaron wrapped an arm around him. "You do have a mommy, son. She lives in Heaven."

"But she can't talk to us or hug us or tell us night-night stories or make us coloring pages. And we can't snuggle on her lap or help her sneak Mina's taters. She can't give us extra cartoon time when we share and don't fight or tattle or wrestle or roughhouse. And she can't throw us balls or take us fishin' or teach us Bible verses and tell us we do a good job."

Braden sat on his knees. "Or build Lego castles with us and make sheet forts on the chairs or do loud music with the Hokey Pokey and take us outside to play and give us reward tickets when we help and obey. Or sneak us sugar snacks or sing to us even though she sings very, very bad."

It didn't escape Aaron's notice that everything they'd mentioned was everything Sarah did. Including sing badly.

"We love our Heaven-mommy. But we want an Earth-mommy, too." Braden's feet scissored against the couch.

Braden tapped his foot on the floor. "Daddy, when's our birthday party?"

"One week from today."

"Yay! Daddy, I wish we could have a new mommy for our birthday. Or for Christmas this year."

"Me, too!" Bryce blinked. "Daddy, is that bad?"

"No, son. It's not bad to want." His nose burned as if he could cry. He never wanted his sons to hurt or want for anything. Especially not the mom they'd never know this side of Heaven. But loss didn't leave anyone in this life alone.

But the same God who allowed it was the God of all hope.

It's not bad to want.

What about me, Lord? Is it bad for me to want another wife?

Is it bad to want Sarah to be that wife?

The more he thought about Sarah, the more the unique wonders of this woman slid across his mind.

Easygoing.

Gentle way about her.

Her walk like a fluid dance.

Contagious laugh.

Appealing.

The kind of unfading beauty that the Bible spoke of. Though she struggled with church attendance at the moment, he knew that would be temporary and that she had a sound relationship with God through private worship, prayer and Bible reading.

His eyes slid across the room. To the photo.

And something shifted. For once it became more a visual reminder to his sons of their mom rather than a reminder of what he'd lost in a mate and in a future that crumbled in the deadly blink of a drunken eye.

He found his gaze disengaging from the frame of glass much easier than the past said he should.

For the first time in years, his lungs could take a grief- and guilt-free breath. How long had it been since tears over Donna had touched his eyes? He could recall days when tears were too plentiful to count and hopelessness dictated his day. Lately though, days devoid of pain became his new norm. And joy had once again taken his heart and home by storm.

Thank You, Lord, for bringing her here. No matter how it ends up.

The thought of a permanent, solid future with Sarah entered his mind. One that had nothing to do with her being the nanny. And everything to do with her completing his limping three-legged family.

A sense of excitement over having something to look forward to awakened like a parachute pluming open. Loving and being loved didn't make life, but it made life more bearable.

He placed a gentle hand on each of his boys, not wanting to make empty promises, yet needing to instill hope to their soul-starved longing. Longing they had not the ability to fulfill.

But the God of all hope could. And if Aaron's heart, being human, nearly ripped at the want in their eyes, how much more would God's heart be moved at the want in his sons' hearts?

"I know, and God knows, how important it is to you

to have another Earth-mommy. Maybe one day, if it's in God's plans, you will. God has a way of working hard things for our good."

Chapter Thirteen

"This will never work." Aaron looked from the occupied pet cage to the outlaw who'd just carried it in the morning of the boys' fourth birthday party. "Ash, Sarah is scared of rodents."

A slow smirk transformed Ash's face into something quite amused and slightly sinister. "I know."

Aaron huffed a sigh, which caused the fuzzy creatures to skitter into their purple plastic igloo. Tiny hairs and cage litter flew everywhere. "*What exactly* are they?"

"Guinea pigs."

He folded his arms and issued Ashleigh a disapproving look. "In other words, rodents."

Ignoring his reprimand, she smiled and poked her finger inside the cage and wiggled it, wormlike.

"I sincerely hope you get bit."

"Oh, lighten up. The boys have been wanting a pet."

"If I believed you nobly got them for the boys, I

might be okay with it. But I have a sneaking suspicion you got them because you know Sarah is terrified of rodents. Which means you'll have to take them back to the store."

Ash always bought the twins unique birthday and Christmas gifts and presents before she left the country. He knew she didn't want the boys to forget about her if something happened. Her work was dangerous so Aaron tolerated her spoiling his sons.

But she should have asked Aaron before buying them pets.

If that was what one could call these things.

"You'll have to get something more suitable."

Ash stood and eyed her watch. "Can't. Already told the boys about them. Got a meeting with Stone in an hour, then I need to tend paperwork in my office this week. I'm leaving my stuff here because I'll be back before I have to leave again."

"Where to this time?"

"Not outside the country. But it's a complicated case."

"Fine. But know I'm not happy about this."

She cupped his cheek and patted. "The boys will love them."

"And you will love that this will torment and frighten the nanny."

Ash laughed and grabbed her jacket and rolling briefcase. "You catch on quick." Her smile faded and her face took on a serious look. "On some things."

"And that means?"

No answer.

He trailed her to the door. "Ash, if this is not about Donna then you need to tell me what it is."

"I told you, when I have all my facts straight, you'll know. In the meantime, keep your heart and head above water. You're slipping. See you at the party."

He felt suddenly unsettled. Ash was a master at intimidation. But what had she meant by that? He followed her to the car, intent on getting info out of her. But she was already driving away.

When Aaron returned inside, Sarah was walking a wide berth around the skittering pets. Her gaze flicked to Aaron. "Ash?"

"Ah, yeah. Sarah, I'm sorry about this. I'll clean out the cage and help the boys keep them fed and watered."

"I appreciate that." Despite having a look in her eyes that sat somewhere between anxious and appalled, traces of her hallmark humor resided.

The boys tromped across the floor squealing when they saw the cage and its contents. "Yay! Auntie Ashleigh brought 'em!"

Bryce extended a carrot through the cage slats. Two baby fluff balls erupted in a flurry of activity. Sarah jumped. The pets crawled over and over one another to get to the carrot.

"Watch out, Bryce. They might bite." Sarah looked as if she wanted to step forward but couldn't.

Aaron did. "Don't put your finger in the cage. Just the carrot. Like this." Aaron snapped the treat and handed one half to Braden, the other to Bryce.

"Here," Braden said to his new pet and poked the vegetable stick through the cage, while Bryce's guinea pig nibbled on the other.

Mina entered with the cakes she'd baked. "Guests are arriving. Shall we get ready to rumble?"

"Yay!" Bryce and Braden exclaimed in unison.

Aaron turned to Sarah. "Come help me greet guests?"

"Love to." Sarah warmed at the contact of Aaron's hand on her back as they approached the door.

Once he opened it, at least a dozen sets of eyes blinked at her from the door frame, then at Aaron. Several eyebrows rose as the men, women and two children trickled in.

"This is Bradley, Joel's son," Aaron said, then turned to a little girl. "And this is Reece, Ben's stepdaughter and her mom, Amelia."

The children bounded toward the twins. Celia and Amber followed, pausing to greet Sarah on their way. What had to be the rest of Aaron's team due to their size, stature and military bearing filed in.

Judging by the amused smirks and surprised grins passed to Aaron that he seemed hard-pressed to ignore as guests passed by, Sarah wasn't what they'd expected.

Aaron motioned the men over. Two of them had to be younger than her twenty-nine. Those two grinned widest.

"This is Javier, Manny's son. And Javier's best friend Enrique."

Sarah stuck out her hand.

"Wow. Strong for a girl," Javier said.

"You can let go of her hand now, son," Manny, whom she'd met the day of the bubble debacle, said. He extended a beefy hand and a beautiful smile. "Hi, Sarah. No bubbles this time?"

She laughed. "No, thankfully."

The one who looked as shy as Bryce, only older, stepped forward. "I'm Chance Garrison."

The rest followed, each shaking her hand.

"Nice to see you again, Sarah." Joel Montgomery, whom she'd also met before, smiled and moved toward the hub of the party.

The tallest, cutest Asian man she'd ever seen stepped forward. "Ben Dillinger. And since they're too humble to say it, Joel's our team leader and Aaron's our commander."

She smiled and waited for the next guy.

"Nolan Briggs," the one with compassionate blue eyes, said then smiled at the lady on his arm. "This is Mandy."

"Brockton Drake." An endearing flush that matched the hair on his head crept across his face as she took his hand. This one didn't wear a wedding band. Nor did the next. Nor had Chance.

"Reardon," the tall, dark and brooding one said. He let his gaze linger long enough that Aaron cleared his throat. "But you can call me Vince. Or just call me."

Joel stepped between them, beating Aaron to the draw. "He's a player, Sarah. Run fast and far."

The men laughed good-naturedly. Tough-as-mortar as they all looked, she felt completely comfortable in their presence. Safe.

Wings of Refuge. What a fitting name for this rescuing military brotherhood. Men led by the most intriguing of them all—at least in her mind. Chief Aaron Petrowski.

She eyed the object of her growing infatuation, then scolded herself. After all, she'd left clues that there were big pieces of the puzzle of her missing. Important pieces that could negate any romantic feelings he had.

"Ready?"

Sarah nodded and followed Aaron to the table. Bryce and Braden, Bradley, Reece and her stuffed brown bear wore pointed party hats.

Aaron set the airplane cake in front of Braden and the helicopter cake in front of Bryce. He lifted a grill lighter toward the candles.

"Wait!" Bryce called out. "We forgot someone!" He scrambled from the table and ran into the family room.

Aaron paused beside her, eyes wide. "Geese?"

Sarah laughed. "Let's hope not. We don't have enough hats or chairs."

His teammates eyed them strangely. Bryce sped back in with a picture frame. *The* picture frame.

Laughter died in Aaron's eyes the same time it died in Sarah's throat. Silence trickled through the room as all eyes assessed Bryce setting the frame bearing Donna's image on the table. "Mommy will want to be here. It is our birthday, after all."

Braden brushed fingers over the frame. "Yeah, now she'll know we're turning four."

Mandy crumbled. Ash slipped from the room. Celia intercepted her. Mina's hand came to her mouth. Men swallowed. Amber and Amelia blinked back tears. The room quieted. No one really knew what to do or say. Uncharacteristically stunned, Aaron put his hands on the back of the chair he stood behind and leaned forward, swallowing hard, looking on the verge of tears.

His team gathered around and put hands of support on his shoulders and back. Aaron's jaw tensed. He bent forward.

Bryce eyed all the adults including his dad. "What? What'd I do?"

Sarah leaned in and rested a hand on Bryce's. "Nothing, sweetie. Daddy just misses Mommy, is all. And he wishes she could be here in person today."

"Me, too. But I'm glad you're here, Miss Sarah."

Braden perked up. "Yeah. You're almost like having a mom."

"Thank you, guys. There's nowhere else in the world I'd rather be than here with you."

"Me and Bryce?"

"Yes. And with your dad."

Aaron lifted his face. Sarah could tell unshed tears had touched his eyes. They now roved over her face as he considered her words. Her very intentional words.

Aaron's teammates and friends bounced gazes back and forth between them. She didn't care. Didn't care who all knew she'd fallen head over heels for all three.

In fact, as she met guests' gazes, all she saw were dawning grins and curious, thankful eyes. Except Ashleigh, who stood alone in the corner, seething. And Sarah knew without a doubt that whatever issue Ash had with her was about to come to a head.

Thankfully, Sarah knew Ash loved the boys enough not to unleash it at their party.

Aaron, whom she respected for having subdued his jolted emotions for the boys' sake, hugged them light-heartedly and lit the candles. "Shall we make wishes and open gifts?"

The boys' faces brightened above the flames. "Yeah!"

After the birthday party guests left, Sarah started to clean up. Skittering noises and squeaks abounded. She eyed the creatures from across the room and cringed. For the twins' sake, she'd try to get along with the little vermin—err—the pigs. And for Aaron's sake, she'd keep trying to get along with Ashleigh. Though she was one coldhearted woman and might negate Sarah's efforts to the end. Sarah wouldn't leave this family without a fight.

A warm hand rested on her shoulder. "Sarah?"

Aaron. Strength poured through his hand as he squeezed her shoulder. Took everything in her not to lean into his touch. She turned her head to see the face that dominated her dreams.

"Yes?"

"Look, I didn't know Ash was going to do it." He gestured to the cage. "In fact, I can't believe she did."

Sarah didn't know from where it came, but she laughed. "I can."

Aaron looked for a moment as if he could laugh. "You're being a good sport about everything." His gaze changed. Grew direct. His hand slid from her shoulder. "Although she doesn't normally act like this toward a person without reason. Good reason."

"Aaron, I know Ash is your sister, but she's wrong about me."

"Are you asking for the benefit of the doubt?"

"Yes."

"Why won't you come to church?"

"If it'll help you trust me, I will."

"When?" He brushed bangs out of her eyes.

"This weekend."

He dropped his hand but his eyes lingered. "Okay. Shall we rescue Mina from the boys?"

Mention of it broke the lovely trance. She enjoyed these snippets she and Aaron had, thanks to Mina giving them time to talk. The woman must have a hoard of Cupid's arrows hidden somewhere.

Sunday morning, Sarah dabbed her eyes as the message touched her heart. The pastor talked about how Jesus' love for humanity drove him to the cross with no guarantee we'd ever love Him back. Then Ben played a worship song he'd written with similar words. Sarah renewed her covenant with God to keep coming to church.

Monday morning Sarah headed downstairs to find

Aaron making iced tea in the kitchen. "Hey." Her face flushed at the mere sight of him.

"Hey. Want to take the boys fishing then help me in the yard?" Aaron asked. "Mina's napping."

"Sure. I'll help the boys on with play clothes."

Aaron grinned. "Already done. They're waiting with tackle boxes by the door." He poured a second glass of tea. For her? He reached for the sugar canister and put two spoonfuls in the glass. Yep. Definitely for her. Aaron didn't drink sweet tea and he didn't like the boys to drink it either. That he'd noticed how much sugar she normally put in hers caused a sweet, giddy feeling to swirl in her the same way Aaron's spoon chased particles around her glass. He poured it into a Thermos cup and handed it to her.

After driving to the edge of Refuge and fishing at a pond Aaron explained was Amber's parents', they returned home for lunch.

Once finished, they retreated outside. They worked alongside one another, laughing and talking and helping the boys stack decorative gray brick edging.

"Anyone want more to drink?" Sarah said, rising after a couple solid hours.

Bryce stood and brushed mulch off his jeans. "Yeah, I'm thirsty."

"And tired." Braden set the spade in the potting soil.

Aaron placed one hand on each of their heads. "Landscaping wears one out. But the beauty in the yard is worth all this work."

As was time spent with Aaron. She cherished every moment granted with him and the boys. But it was nice to have alone time with each, including Aaron. He seemed to feel the same.

"I'll grab some bottles of water." Aaron headed inside.

Back outside, he sat next to Sarah on the porch swing while Bryce and Braden played in the yard. Swinging leisurely, she and Aaron talked about life and faith and everything in between.

Everything except what had become to her the most important thing. *Give me a chance to share my past with Aaron.*

"I'll take care of the boys' baths," Aaron said as they all came back inside.

"Okay. I'll be upstairs if anyone needs something." Sarah ascended the stairs, entered her room and sat at her desk. No doubt that God would answer her prayer and give her the chance to reveal her past. *Give me courage to seize that chance.*

No doubt that God would answer that prayer, too.

Question was, would Aaron react like Ashleigh claimed?

And give him the grace to accept me in spite of it and know that I've truly changed. Sarah laughed. *In short, I'm asking You to help him hear Your voice above his sister's. I know You love her and of course Aaron loves her. But…* "We both know how loud Ash can be when she wants to be heard."

"Sarah?"

She jerked. Aaron stood at her bedroom door.

She removed her hand from her throat. "Y-yes?"

One corner of his mouth curved up. "Talking to yourself?"

"Uh—no. I just didn't hear you come up."

"I knocked. You were pretty lost in thought there. Everything okay?"

"Yeah, everything's—"

Give me a chance…

Duh. Her chance had tromped right up here and was staring her in the face.

Sarah turned her chair around. "Actually, things aren't exactly okay."

His forehead creased. "You're still happy here, right? I mean, I know there's been a touch of tension between you and Ash."

"A touch?" Sarah laughed. "Don't you mean a ton?"

"You have a point."

She drew a breath. "Sit down, Aaron. There's something hard that I need to tell you."

He studied her a moment. Then pushed his sleeves up. "I'm all ears."

No, actually he was all muscles, but that was the last thing she should be noticing right now.

Her throat dried of all moisture, probably because it routed to the palms of her hands. She drew a deep breath. "Aaron, I've been wanting to tell you that—"

His pager went off.

Peering at it, he straightened. "Sorry, I need to call Joel. He never pages this number unless we have a mission."

Cell out, Aaron stepped into the hall.

Sarah let out a long-suffering breath. Eyed the ceiling. "Does this mean now's not the right time?"

Moments later Aaron reemerged. Four long strides took him across the floor. "The team's been tasked to a disaster in the States. I'm going with. Be home in a few days." He bent and kissed her on the cheek. Then jerked back, surprising them both.

He looked utterly confused a moment, same way she felt. "I—uh, have no idea why that happened. Just seemed the thing to do." He stepped backward and hiked a thumb toward her door. "We'll continue this when I return in a few days."

And just like that, he disappeared.

Just what did he mean to continue? The conversation she'd initiated? Or the spontaneous kiss he'd planted on her cheek as though it was the most natural thing to do?

Well, doubtful he'd ever do that again after she finished telling him what she should have told him from the start.

Chapter Fourteen

What had she been about to say?

The thought trailed Aaron into the house days later. He returned from his mission to find the boys napping and Mina in the kitchen. "How long they been asleep?"

Mina wielded a wicked-looking vegetable peeler. "Not long enough for you to go wake them up. Unless you want to deal with the wrath."

"Uh, no. Think I'll pass." Though he'd missed them, Mina was right. There'd be double meltdown if he woke them before their bodies had rested enough.

"How'd your mission go?"

"Excellent. We rescued many civilians and animals from roofs along the Mississippi. A levee broke, flooding an area around Elizabethtown."

"I'm glad you're back in the swing of things. The boys actually did okay with you being gone. Sarah kept them highly entertained."

Speaking of— "Where is she?" They had yet to complete their conversation, and talk about why he'd given her a goodbye kiss. He wasn't really sure himself yet.

"Upstairs writing one of her letters."

"I wonder who she writes to." He leaned against the counter and studied Mina.

"Shame on you, Aaron. But I admit I wonder that, too. I sneaked a peek at the address, in fact."

He snorted. "And you call *me* nosey."

"Well, aren't you gonna ask me where the letters go?"

He grabbed an apple and bit into it. "Nope. It's really none of our business."

"Really?"

"Really." Though admittedly this whole letter thing and the mystery surrounding Saturday nights bugged him and begged to be solved. Aaron tossed the apple in the air and caught it. After polishing one off, he reached for a second.

"Hey, I was saving those to teach Sarah how to make Amber's Mountain Dew apple dumplings."

"I noticed lately Sarah's been learning how to cook and letting you lead those lessons."

"Um-hm." She looked as if she harbored a secret.

He stared at the apples in the bowl and thought about all the calories in Amber's dumplings. "They're healthier this way. Without all that sugar."

Everyone in the house knew Aaron's rigid anti-sugar stance. He didn't want the boys to have sweets at all. Yet he knew very well Mina and Ash snuck candy to the boys. And now Sarah had joined the ranks of doling out sugar.

"Besides, you need a little something to sweeten you up."

"Have I been grumpy lately?"

"I'll say. What's going on, Aaron?"

He leaned over the counter and set the uneaten apple back in the wooden fruit bowl. "Haven't slept well."

"And of course you never sleep in. You get up the same time every day. Oh-dark-thirty."

He grinned. "I'm on military time, remember?" Plus, he liked to work out and run while the sun and the world still slept.

"Yeah, so why haven't you been sleeping?"

"Been trying to come up with solutions on how to bring my teams together in Refuge to better help the community." Not to mention a certain nanny kept his mind occupied until the wee hours, facing the unfinished emotional business they'd both started when he'd been tasked to a mission.

"Among other things, I need to get to the root of Ash's dislike of her. It's starting to concern me."

"For Sarah's safety?"

Aaron laughed because he knew Mina was serious. "No. Ash wouldn't hurt her. Unless she thought Sarah would hurt the boys."

Mina shot up like someone a third of her age. "That's absurd. Sarah would never hurt a child. I'm telling you, Ash has a hang-up because she was so close to Donna."

"That's what I thought at first, too. Now I'm not so sure."

"Well, I am sure. As long and hard as we've prayed, God would tell us if we needed to be wary of Sarah. God loves those little boys even more than you do, Aaron. Trust God to protect your sons. And don't let Ashleigh's cold heart keep yours from finding joy in what's obviously blooming between you and Sarah."

The apple must have gone down wrong because he had difficulty swallowing all of a sudden. Yet he knew it was useless to refute. "On the safety issue, I pray you're right, Mina. Because bad things happen to good people all the time."

Her dark brows rose. "And what about the other issue?"

He knew she meant her indication that romantic things were blooming between him and Sarah. "I can't focus on that until I get to the bottom of Ash's ire toward Sarah. There must be something to it. One way or another, I'm going to find out." A hard three-person confrontation might be on the horizon.

She pulled the lid off the sugar canister. "I understand. By the way…it's the courthouse."

Aaron turned. "What?"

"The letters. She mails them to a courthouse in Kentucky."

"How do you know?"

"Ash told me this morning. I had her look up the address. She visited Sarah's town. But that's all she would say."

Sarah's note cards seemed almost an obsessive compulsion. He wanted to solve the mystery. But didn't want to invade her privacy. A part of him hoped she'd feel safe enough in their friendship to offer up the information on her own.

Maybe that's what she'd wanted to talk to him about. Who would a single woman in her late twenties mail a homemade letter to three days a week? Strange indeed. A horrible thought hit him—he hoped she wasn't corresponding with a criminal. Yet he rarely saw her get domestic mail. Then again, it wasn't as if he went snooping through her stuff. "Maybe it's something as innocent as her having a relative in jail or something."

"It's killing you to know. So why don't you just ask her?"

"Think I will."

"And if she doesn't tell you?"

"She doesn't tell me."

"And you go digging on your own?"

"Maybe. If I feel the need to for her safety or ours." Until then, he'd leave it alone. If Sarah needed protection, Ash could and would help her, despite her hard feelings. Either way, they had to clear the air.

He walked up the stairs and knocked on her door. "Sarah?"

Shuffling sounded, then he heard the closing of a drawer. "In here, just a sec." Her voice came closer then the door opened. She wore a light gray gym outfit with pink stripes down the sleeves and the legs. The colors complemented her complexion.

"Getting ready to work out?"

"Just did. Your mission went well?"

"Very. May I come in?"

She stepped back, smiling. "It's your house."

"But this is your room."

"Not technically."

"Yes, technically. For as long as you want it."

"I have no plans to leave anytime soon."

He eyed the letter in progress and felt a twinge of jealousy for the recipient of her lovingly crafted cards. "Not even for whoever you send those letters to?"

Her face paled then turned red. Her eyebrows pinched together in a scowl. "It's not what you think."

He leaned against the doorjamb and grinned. "And what do I think?"

"Well, I have no idea. I suppose you think I'm writing a beau."

"A beau?" A laugh slipped out. "As in a beau who comes a courtin'?"

Her flabbergasted look caused by his teasing words propelled him closer.

She smacked his arm playfully, but he caught her hand in his and held it. "I just want you safe, Sarah." *I want you with me.*

The strength of his own thought startled him.

"I'm safe. Promise."

He released her arm. "Sure?"

"Absolutely."

He eyed the card-making paraphernalia. "You'd be a great asset to Celia, Amber, Amelia and Mandy's soldier care-package program."

"They stopped by a few times to take me to a coffeehouse with them."

Aaron was glad his team's women were reaching out to Sarah. "You could make a homemade card for each box. I'd supply the items necessary, if you like."

"I'd love to get involved in the care packages. But I'd like to pay for the items myself. My employer pays me well." Her face transformed. What a smile. The room telescoped.

He tugged at the neck of his shirt. What was the thermostat set at in here anyway? Seven hundred degrees?

"Can we talk? Or should I let you get back to your letter-writing?"

She grew quiet. "We need to talk. But the boys will be up soon." And she looked as if she needed to regather her nerve to say whatever she had to.

"We'll take a rain check, then. See you at dinner." He turned to go, casting one last look at her desk. "You don't have much light."

"It's enough."

"Could be why you're getting those headaches."

Her eyes widened. "How did you know?"

"Mina."

Sarah twisted the cap off her water bottle.

"She also told me the letters go to a courthouse."

"I think I feel violated. But I assure you I'm not

doing anything illegal or immoral." Bottle lifted, she took a swig.

"I hope you're not writing an inmate. That's very dangerous."

Jerked forward, she spewed. Tears filled her eyes with the laughter. She wiped water droplets off her mouth.

"I'll take that as a no."

She nodded, giggling.

"See you at dinner."

"You already said that."

"So I did." He left her room and went back downstairs, more confounded than ever. If not an inmate, then who?

She had to tell him. And soon. Sarah dipped her calligraphy pen into the ink and scrolled letters across a parchment card. A sound at her door caused her to pause and look.

Bryce, rubbing his eyes, stood with bright-red cheeks. Oh, no! He looked ill. "Hey, little buddy. You okay?"

He blinked as if to focus, but didn't seem to see her. "Mommy?" His steps wobbled and his eyes had that "lights are on but nobody's home" look as he reached out his arms toward her. "Mommy?" He toddled in place.

Mommy?

She blinked back empathetic tears. Her heart dropped. "It's Sarah, sweetie." Rushing close, she embraced him. "Mama?" He clutched at her and looked on the verge of tears.

"Miss Sarah's here, sweetie." She pulled him closer, feeling his forehead. Sweltering!

He sniveled into her shoulder. "I want Mommy."

I wish I was. Emotion stung Sarah's nose. "You're burning up. Let's get you downstairs." She lifted him and sped. Two steps out the door, Sarah nearly plowed into the brick wall of Aaron.

"I thought I heard him get up." Aaron reached for Bryce but he clung to Sarah.

"Want Mommy."

Aaron's body jerked. His head swerved and their gazes locked.

Sarah swallowed. Then shrugged. "He's feverish and talking out of his head. Let's get him some Tylenol and Pedialyte Freezer pops."

"You're right. He's pretty warm."

"Daddy?"

Aaron reached for him. Bryce, listless, slid into Aaron's arms and let his head fall against Aaron's chest. "Where do you feel bad?"

"In my tummy." He reached for Sarah. "Need Mommy."

Aaron seemed intent to avoid Sarah's gaze. But frankly, she couldn't look away. For the first time ever she saw bonafide tears glistening in Aaron's eyes.

They gave Bryce Tylenol and a sponge bath. Once the fever came down, Aaron lifted Bryce from where he'd fallen asleep on the couch between them. Clingy from not feeling well, Bryce hadn't wanted Sarah or Aaron to leave his side.

"I'll go put him down. He'll rest better in bed. I'll put him in mine so he doesn't infect Braden."

On Aaron's heels, Sarah padded up the stairs with Bryce's comfort blanket, which she just now noticed was covered in geese.

If it were any other time, she'd laugh. The silk corner had an embroidered inscription: *To Bryce— From Daddy. Happy 2nd Birthday*. Sarah wondered which came first, the goose blanket or the imaginary friends it undoubtedly symbolized.

"Sleepy boy, coming in for a landing." Aaron gently placed Bryce in his king-size bed while making slight airplane noises.

Bryce managed a feeble smile. Aaron started to leave. Bryce whimpered. "No, Daddy. Stay."

Aaron cast Sarah an apologetic glance. "We'll have to talk another time."

"I understand. I'll get the light." She left the closet light on but turned off the room light and pulled the door to.

Once again, their talk was suspended by circumstances out of her control or his.

Sarah started down the stairs. Her thoughts turned to God. "Work this out. In every sense of the words. And get Bryce well soon. Amen."

Chapter Fifteen

❧

"Get back here you silly…arrghh!"

Aaron was used to the shrieks of laughter. But this wasn't that kind of sound. He pushed open the front door and stepped into the family room.

And bit back a laugh. Sarah dangled upside down off the front of the couch with her face shoved into the underskirting. A barricade of furniture and boxes surrounded all three sides of the couch except the front.

She wiggled and huffed and swept her hands back and forth beneath the couch skirting.

He stepped farther in, wanting to make his presence known. Obviously she was too preoccupied to notice his arrival.

Wait, something else was wrong. House was way too quiet. "Where are the boys?"

Her face popped up. "With Mina. She drove them to the Cone Zone for a sundae so I could find one of those furry rodents with inch-long teeth that you all claim are pets."

"One got loose?"

"Yes." She huffed, clearly flustered. Something that rarely happened, even while caring for his hyperactive kids. Cheeks an endearing red, her eyes implored, "Help?"

He peeled off his jacket and tossed it onto the chair. Rolled up his sleeves and dropped to his hands and knees. He had hunted down international terrorists and flushed entire armies of militia out of thousands of acres of hidden desert caves. For crying out loud, how hard could it be to get a one-pound, unarmed guinea pig out from underneath a small civilian couch?

An hour later, Aaron was breathing as heavily as Sarah. "Sneaky little fella. And fast."

Sarah pushed herself off the floor and twisted around to sitting. "Tell me about it. I chased him for an hour before you got here."

"I wonder how many grams of sugar from those sundaes the boys have had so far." Aaron let out a disgusted snort.

"I wonder that, too." Sarah snickered then smothered it.

"What's so funny?"

"It's your night with them, and they'll be on a raging sugar high."

Aaron shook his head and took a swig off a bottle of water, then handed it to her.

She eyed it like Bryce eyed fishing worms, which grossed him out. "Uh…"

"Oh, come on, Miss Asepsis. I don't have germs." He nudged her elbow.

"I beg to differ, Mr. Elite Paramedic. Everyone has germs."

"Not me."

She rolled her eyes at him, then the bottle, but tilted it back and swallowed.

"Except those oral ones that can't be cured with antibiotics." Aaron grinned.

A cough sputtered out. She shoved the bottle toward him and swiped her mouth with jerking motions. And that mouth… Suddenly the room shrank. The temperature rose. He reached over, brushed a thumb along her bottom lip.

Her eyes widened, lips parted. No words. But the question shone from her eyes.

What is happening between us?

"You…you…" *Are so beautiful.* "You…ah…missed a spot." Cupping the side of her face, he brushed a thumb over water droplets below her lip, then gently lifted her face using mild pressure of his fingertips on her jawline.

She swallowed and didn't speak. Her breathing was definitely not normal. If this wasn't attraction arcing between them, he'd lost all touch with reality.

"What would a pretty young thing want with an old codger?" His gaze dropped from her eyes to her lips.

She also let her gaze drop to his mouth before darting back to his eyes. "You're no codger."

Aaron cleared his voice and lowered his hand.

She captured it in hers, bringing his hand back to her face. "And I'd want him not to pull his hand away. I kind of liked that there."

"That so?" Aaron's heart rate sped.

His eyes softened into a caress. Powerful arms that had pulled countless accident victims to safety embraced her. Never taking his eyes off her, Aaron closed his mouth over hers, a kiss that curled her toes. As soon as she thought her skin would meld like Play-Doh into his, he pulled back. But only an inch.

He drew a slow breath and his eyes sought hers. "Sarah?" Questions that had nothing to do with the kiss resided in the word.

She leaned into the comfort of his embrace. He kissed her again. Deeper this time, yet still tender and respectful. She felt like she couldn't get close enough, but he continually kept a polite, safe space between them.

Minutes later, she pulled back because she wanted to look at him. Talk about this. But the blue smolder residing in his delightfully dazed eyes when she pulled away said talking was the last thing on his mind. Sarah laughed.

Aaron grinned. "What? My technique rusty or something?" He draped a loose arm around her shoulder as they sat on the floor side by side, backs leaned against the couch.

Laugh choked out, she reached again for his water, and then stopped.

Now Aaron laughed. "It's not like we haven't just swapped major germs, Sarah."

Her skin heated at his gentle reference to the kiss.

"So I think it's all right if you drink after me."

"I just, I got mono once in high school."

"From kissing?" A teasing glint entered his eyes.

She laughed. "No. From drinking after people. It made me miss a lot of school."

"Hmm. Nice." His eyes dropped back to her mouth, causing her to doubt he'd even heard her at all. She'd never seen that degree of interest flare in a man's eyes before.

"I think I'd like to kiss you again," he murmured.

It scared and thrilled her at the same time. "I—I think we should look for the rat."

Aaron's arm tightened around her. "I think he'll come out when he's good and hungry."

Before Sarah could form a protest, Aaron pulled her close and dipped his head.

The door banged open, and two boys burst through the room.

Sarah jerked away from Aaron and scrambled to sitting.

"I tried to call but no one—" Mina screeched in her tracks. Eyed Aaron. Eyed Sarah. Eyed their surroundings, then raised her brows.

She knew!

Sarah looked around. What gave them away? Well, technically they'd only kissed, but mercy, what a kiss.

Aaron's deliriously supercharged expression had to

be the biggest clue. Even worse, she was trembling like a schoolgirl skipping class. And Aaron looked as if he had nothing in the world to be ashamed about. His face contained nothing except a smug, telltale grin that blared he was quite pleased with himself. Or maybe just quite pleased.

"Oops. Am I interrupting something?" A matronly smile lifted Mina's mouth. "Something important, perhaps?"

Aaron grinned. "Yes. Definitely." He pointed to the door. "Go back to the Cone Zone and get the boys another sundae or two or ten."

Mina's brows rose farther. "This coming from the man who banned sugar from the house? He's smitten," Mina said while shooing the boys to the bathroom.

Face heating, Sarah followed Mina. "We—we were trying to rescue the MIA rodent."

"Right." Mina covered her mouth, but snickers prevailed.

Cause lost, Sarah retreated, avoiding Aaron's piercing gaze and gentle grin as he reached under the couch and produced a docile guinea pig.

What on earth?

He put the animal back in its cage.

Sarah tried to straighten her hair before the boys came back from flooding the bathroom and noticed it out of place. Speaking of, where was her barrette? Had it fallen out? She bent, scanning the floor around the couch.

Grinning, Aaron extended his arm and opened his hand. "Looking for this?"

The barrette!

She gasped and snatched it from him. Heat flushed her face.

"I like it down." His gaze brushed her hair.

He'd released her hair? When?

The man could time-warp her to another world.

Grasping her hands in his, Aaron pulled her effortlessly close. "No need to feel ashamed."

Mina walked back in just then. Sarah tried to pull back. Aaron's firm grip made that impossible. Sarah tugged hard and he released her with reluctance. She moved across the room. He stayed put other than to lift his strong chin and grin.

As Mina looked from one to the other, a curious look came to her face.

Sarah approached the housekeeper. "I—I know this looks inappropriate and I hope you don't get the wrong idea."

"Wrong idea? Honey, there is nothing inappropriate about falling in love with a man like Aaron." Mina headed off as though walking in on the nanny and the employer kissing was the most normal thing in the world.

Unless Mina no longer saw Sarah as the nanny. Sarah still saw herself that way. Did Aaron? If not, she didn't need to live here. Twinges of guilt pinched at her right now for allowing that particular affection, though wholesome, to happen while she was on duty.

But then again, when wasn't she on duty? Only nights when Aaron had Daddy time with the boys, which was technically tonight. She chanced a peek at him, only to find him still staring with that open grin.

"What?"

He shook his head. "You." The word didn't carry criticism, but affection. And the tender look in his eyes melted her insides. He cared. Deeply. This wasn't about the physical attraction they'd both battled lately.

This was something more. Mina had called it falling in love. Come to think of it, Aaron hadn't disputed the statement.

Air whooshed from her lungs as she looked at the man whose eyes seemed to beckon forever in hers.

Did she love Aaron Petrowski?

Yes.

Did he love her back? She studied his face. If his expression and the deep longing there were indicators… yes.

But would he feel the same when he discovered her past?

Dread swept through her at the thought of his reaction.

Because she couldn't possibly know the answer.

Not until she told him the truth.

Please, give me courage.

A thought came to her. Her plans to tell Aaron had been continually thwarted.

Maybe she needed to start with Ashleigh.

Chapter Sixteen

Sarah drew a deep breath, dreading this conversation. "May I talk to you?" She moved inside the doorway of the bedroom Ash slept in during times she stayed here.

"Suit yourself." Ash stabbed the remote at the TV. The sharp motion reminded Sarah of a swordfighting maneuver.

"I want to talk about the items you put in my room."

Ash swung her feet over the bed and sat up in one swift motion. Sarah fought the urge to scramble back.

Though they remained across the room from one another, Ash's superior height and uncensored expressions of disdain and displeasure made it feel as though she was towering over Sarah. "You don't know what I do for a living, do you?"

Ash hadn't invited her in and it didn't feel safe to tread, so Sarah stayed at the door. "No."

"I make people disappear. People in danger. Give

them a new identity and a new life." She narrowed her gaze to a glare. "I also dig up dirt on others. Especially those who are a menace to society."

"What do you mean?"

"I started out as a P.I. But now, I'm an international government skip tracer. Aaron had me run a check on you."

"I don't know what a skip tracer is."

"Among other things, we find people who have attempted to disappear. We track down fugitives. We find sanctuary for endangered witnesses." Ash drilled her with a penetrating look that strikingly resembled Aaron's. Definitely twins.

"And most important, at least where you're concerned, we can find anything out about anyone, anywhere, anytime, present…or past." Ash stepped closer. Her expression softened, but only marginally. "Interestingly, I took a trip to Kentucky recently. Talked to some folks from your hometown."

Sarah put quaky, clammy hands against the doorjamb. "So you know."

"Of course I do. Question is, does Aaron? I'm betting no. Because if he did, you would never have been hired."

"It was an accident." All power had left Sarah's voice.

"Drinking and driving? No. It's a choice. A crime. And a killer of innocent people."

The words thrust invisible swords through Sarah's middle. She nearly doubled over. Did Ashleigh know something about Sarah's accident that Sarah didn't?

Had the child she hit ended up not surviving?

Had she written all these letters in vain?

Worse, had she ripped a child from the arms of parents who so solemnly loved her?

A swift sinking sensation pulled Sarah toward the tile. The floor grew wobbly beneath her feet. She braced her hand against the wall. Ash stepped forward; a flash of uncharacteristic concern—very short-lived, yet there nonetheless—darted across her face. Wonder of wonders. Then the usual hatred covered it.

Sarah held Ash's gaze. "I don't drink anymore."

"Moot point. You do realize he's going to hate you when he finds out?"

Her hands quaked. "H-hate me? Why?"

"Get a clue, sister. Ask Mina to tell you how Aaron's wife died. In the meantime, prepare to look for another job."

Ash's words struck terror in Sarah. "W-what do you mean, ask how she died? I don't understand what that has to do with me."

"It has everything to do with you." Ash hulked nose to nose over Sarah. "I don't like you because I don't like people who don't consider the safety of other people. And neither does Aaron. And for good reason."

What Ash said after that, Sarah had no idea. Her mind whirled in a sickening vortex of dread and hard questions. Questions she didn't think she could handle the answers to. She faltered back and ran down the stairs, fighting nausea and tears. How did she die? Oh, God. Lord Jesus. How did she die?

Yet everything in her knew.

Sarah stopped at the kitchen, leaning over the trash can until she was sure she wouldn't get sick.

Ash blew past her. "You've no right to this family."

She couldn't breathe, she couldn't breathe, she couldn't breathe. "Oh, God. I should have told him," she prayed.

"Told him what?" Mina came into the kitchen.

Sarah lifted her face, but sound refused to surface.

"What did Ash say to you? Because she can be a bully, you know. She's hunted down terrorists before. Don't let her get to you."

But the words hardly registered, much less made sense or took root.

Sarah stumbled to the living room to stare at the picture. She ran trembling fingers along the glass, cradling an image of a face that held a hint of Braden's dimples and the slope of Bryce's nose.

How did you die?

But she knew the answer before she could ask. Oh, God, no. She didn't want to know. She had to know. Sarah plucked the picture with moist palms and held it to her queasy stomach. Then brought it to her pounding heart. Her eyes bled sorrow all over the frame.

Mina came up behind her. "Sarah, what's going on?"

Sarah turned, tears still dripping on the glass as she held it out to look at Bryce and Braden's mother, and the woman Aaron had loved enough to marry. "Mina, h-how exactly did she die?"

"She was hit and killed by a drunk driver."

Her world tumbled. Glass shattered around Sarah's feet and the room drifted far from focus. Her arms flailed to keep herself from falling.

Someone shaking her brought sharp edges and sound back into the room. Focus. Focus. Don't pass out. But her knees crumbled anyway.

"I'm sorry," she said to the broken frame. No idea why. Whether it had to do with how Donna died or that she was the kind of person who caused it. Or whether her sorrow burst out over the broken glass. A precious memento. And she'd just shattered it. Like she'd shattered that little girl and her family. She couldn't begin to measure how much she'd grown to love Bryce and Braden more than anything on earth could measure. And how they desperately longed for their mom.

And she was exactly what took her from them.

"Oh, God. Help me please. Mina, I'm going to be sick."

"Sarah! Sarah! What's wrong?" Mina helped her to sitting. "Here. Put your head between your knees."

She drew deep breaths, realizing she'd come close to passing out again. The urge to throw up receded. The floor still felt unsteady, but she was now sitting. She bent her knees toward her. Crunching sounded under her feet. She blinked her eyes open.

"Oh, no!" Sarah stared at the four severed pieces and the shards of glass and felt just like the frame—

completely shattered. She reached forward, wanting nothing more than to put it all back together. Not just the frame and not just today. Her stream of bad choices that had led to that terrible day.

Desperation caused Sarah to heave forward and gather the broken pieces in her hands. Could this be fixed? Never. But she had to try. She scooped the pieces up, despite Mina blocking and pulling at her hands. Numb. Everything—numb. In and out of focus. Voices. Murmuring. Spanish. Prayers. Mina?

"Don't move. You'll get cut." A male voice, coming closer. Oh, God. Aaron. What must he think? What must he have endured in the way of having to forgive someone for the crime that took his wife? She moved her face to meet his gaze. His jaw tensed, but he wasn't looking at the picture. He was looking at her. He stepped over the beloved memento she'd broken and dropped to Sarah's side.

"I—I broke everything."

Confusion and concern entered his face.

"Here." Mina swept around Sarah's feet as Sarah lifted them.

"What happened?" Aaron looked to Mina, then parked his gaze on Sarah.

Something in Spanish. Then in English, "I don't know!" Spanish. Spanish. "We were just talking and she wavered and went down." More Spanish. Aaron seemed to understand every word.

At a break in Mina's panicked babble, he eyed Sarah. "What happened?"

She eyed the frame. "I'm sorry. I guess I just dropped it."

He shook his head. "No. That's not entirely it."

Oh, God. *God. His wife died from what I used to be.* Mental prayers. Desperate. She needed air. Couldn't tell him. He'd fire her, rightfully, and the boys, she'd never see them again. Or Mina. Or Aaron.

At the thought her heart shattered like the glass, into four pieces, one for each person she'd never get to see again. For each jagged piece symbolized someone her heart had come to love yet would have to leave.

Served her right. Macy's mother's declaration that day in court was coming true.

"Sarah?" Aaron waited for an answer, and clearly, he wasn't waiting patiently.

"It was a shock to know, to hear how she died." Not a lie.

Aaron studied her carefully and pressed his fingers into her wrist. "Do you have low blood sugar?"

"No."

"Known medical problems?"

She shook her head. "I lost hold of the frame. It dropped."

Mina shook her head and braced Sarah's shoulders. "No, *mija, you* nearly dropped. Not just the frame. Right after I told you that—" Mina stopped abruptly, studied her. Careful understanding dawned. Mina darted a quick glance at Aaron. "Right after we talked about all the chores we needed to do. Come on. Let's get you to bed. You need rest. Aaron will clean up the glass."

"I'm fine. Really." Not really. Far from fine. Aaron didn't deserve to have to pick up the broken pieces. Not of the frame and not of losing someone because of someone else's selfish actions. Precisely why Ash was right. Sarah didn't deserve to be in this home right now. And she'd just destroyed the only trinket Aaron had kept out in plain view of his wife.

Worse, she could have been the one to have taken her life.

Mina dragged Sarah to the bedroom, Spanish streaming out.

"I can't understand a word you're saying," Sarah said.

"Yes, but the good Lord can. Sit. Sit. Tell me why you really dropped the frame," she whispered, dabbing Sarah's forehead with a cool cloth.

Sarah's gaze dropped to the ground.

"Sarah?"

"I'm sorry. I just can't." Sobs threatened to claim her throat.

"Yes, you can. I won't tell. We're friends and you need to get this off your chest. You're as white as Aaron's legs in winter."

She wished she could have laughed at that.

"Do you have an alcohol problem?"

Sarah shook her head. "Not anymore."

Mina lowered herself to the bed. "But you did?"

Tears came despite her best efforts to stop them. "Yes."

"Did you hurt someone?"

"Yes." Raw.

"The letters you write. Is that to the person you hurt?"

She nodded because her throat had closed.

"Did the person live?"

"I don't know." Tortured. "At first she did. But I haven't heard from her. Something might have happened since the trial."

She expected Mina to storm downstairs and tell Aaron, then both of them to demand she leave immediately.

But instead Mina wrapped strong arms around her and held her tightly. She rocked back and forth and let a Spanish lullaby float around them. Sarah was sure Mina also prayed for her. She couldn't understand the words, but Mina was right.

God could.

"We don't need to tell him yet. It's close to what would have been the anniversary. Now would be a bad time."

"But I need to tell him."

"Yes. But I suggest you wait. Plus, he's leaving for two weeks to oversee training operations with his three PJ teams. You can tell him when he returns. If he gets mad, I'll double his dessert for six months until he sweetens up."

"We all know Aaron doesn't do dessert."

"Well, I'll think of something to soften him."

"I'll lose my job. The boys, Mina, they've become so much more than a job to me. So have you. And Aaron…"

"You've grown to care for him, no?"

"How do you say 'major understatement' in Spanish?"

Mina chuckled. "God will work this out."

"How do you know He won't work this out by working me out of your lives?"

"Because I know He sent you here. Aaron and I both feel that way."

"But I've always had a nagging sense that God would repay my deed with a loss as equal."

"Why would you think that when Jesus already took your punishment? You've got punishment and consequence mixed up. And, baby girl, you have paid the consequences dearly with living your life in fear of retribution."

"How can I live any other way when I don't know how she is or what kind of life she's had?"

"Are you saying His blood wasn't enough? *Mija,* you are insulting His sacrifice. No, no, no. He is enough, more than enough."

"Maybe He brought me here to punish me."

"Maybe He brought you here to bless you as much as you bless us?"

"I can't wrap my mind around that."

"You need to."

"But Ash hates me. And rightfully so."

"No. I beg to differ. True, Ash doesn't like you, but I feel it's wrongfully so."

"Still—I don't deserve to be a mother. Macy's mom even said so in court. That if I ever had children—they'd suffer for my actions."

"Ah-ah. You've got way wrong thinking about Him and about yourself. We're going to start praying that God sets you right in your perception. And frees you from this prison of fear and vows of sentencing yourself to never be a mother. Thinking you don't deserve children or if you have them, someone will do to them what you did to that child, is utter bunk."

Sarah drew a breath. Sniffed and dabbed her nose. "I don't know anymore, Mina."

"Have you taken a drink since?"

"No."

"Do you plan to?"

"No. I'd die first."

"Don't talk like that."

"I can't help it." She faced her friend. "Mina, if I have to leave this family, my life is over."

At Mina's sharp gasp, Sarah knew she should clarify. "I'd never try to end my life. That's not what I meant."

"Then what?"

"If Ashleigh gets her way and I am forbidden to see the boys, or you or Aaron, I'll be devastated."

Yet wasn't that what she'd told herself all her life she deserved? To have something precious taken from her as retribution for her actions?

Maybe her reckoning had come?

Tears filled her eyes and emotion clogged her throat. "If I never got to see you all again, I'd live my days an empty shell."

"No, *mija*. Things will not go that way. God has a

plan and a hope for you. And hope does not disappoint."

"I don't deserve the right to hope. I gave it up when I got in that car. My attorney wanted me to plead not guilty. I couldn't. I never understand why criminals care more about serving less time than owning up to their wrongs."

"You're not a criminal."

"Yes, Mina. I am a convicted criminal because I hurt a child. Because I was a juvie and a first-time DUI offender, my records were sealed. But that doesn't make me innocent. I'm guilty of DUI and bodily harm. Guilty of the same actions that took his wife from this life and from him and from their babies."

"Aaron won't see you that way."

Yet flickers of fear and a dash of doubt in Mina's eyes alluded otherwise.

"But God's future for me may hold no hope of remaining with this family."

That Mina didn't refute it only confirmed how sickeningly close her fears were of coming true.

Chapter Seventeen

"Everything still a go tonight?" Mina closed the dishwasher.

"Yes. It's been a month since the frame broke," Sarah said. Though he'd returned two weeks ago, Aaron had spent the past three days at the DZ. "No more putting it off. I need to tell him. Should have already."

Mina patted her apron. "Don't live in regret. Move forward and be determined to do your best from here. Let me know when he arrives from the DZ and I will take the boys to Joel and Amber's to play with Bradley. They're expecting us for dinner. You did great with Aaron's dinner, by the way."

"Thank you. Of course he'll know I'm trying to soften him up."

"Honey, believe me, garlic potatoes and pot roast are the way to that man's heart. Not that you need help in that department."

"What are you inferring?"

"No inferring about it. That man is sweet as sugar on you."

"Not that it will matter after today. Besides, Aaron's not keen on sugar."

"Trust. Remember?"

Sarah nodded. "I need to blow off some nervous steam. Why don't you rest while I take the boys outside to play?"

"Excellent idea. Why don't you go ahead and wear them completely out while you're at it? Make my job ten times easier."

The women laughed together, then parted ways. Sarah took the boys outside to help her finish up with last-minute details on the yard she'd slaved over for the past few days in Aaron's absence.

If she was going to leave this home, she was going to leave it beautiful. Yard and all.

"Come on, boys. Let's go outside and play until your daddy gets home."

And I have to face the music.

She soaked up every single second with the boys and prayed they weren't her last.

Mina approached. "Aaron just called. He's on his way home. The boys will want to attack him with hugs and chatter once they see him. So before Aaron arrives, I'll take them to Haven Street park before driving them to dinner."

"Thank you. That'll give us chance to talk."

Sarah helped buckle the boys into Mina's car.

"Owie, you're squishin' me!" Bryce said as she

hugged him, then Braden, enormously tight. Doors shut, the car started off. Panic tore at her as the boys waved at her from the back window.

Please, please don't let this be the last time I see them.

Yet how could she pray that when she might have caused a parent to have to see her child for the last time?

Trust.

At least if Aaron ended up wanting nothing to do with her, she'd made memories to cherish with Bryce and Braden.

Because if Ashleigh ended up being right about Aaron, Sarah would likely never get to see them after this day.

Lord, I don't deserve it. But because Jesus erased my sin with Himself, I'm not asking for memories.

I'm asking for time.

Such a short time!

How had she managed this?

Aaron surveyed his transformed yard as he pulled into the driveway Monday after returning from pararescue training with his teams. Sarah, wearing a ball cap, turned and waved.

Brick paths, shrubs and other greenery that hadn't been in his yard when he left Thursday had given it a botanical facelift. Mina had mentioned on the phone that Sarah had done a little more landscaping and that the yard was taking shape.

"A little landscaping?" The woman was a rockwall wonder. Plants. Rock gardens. Even a bench. For the first time, beauty surrounded his house and dominated his yard. And Sarah outshone all of the fall flowers and yard ornaments combined.

He rolled down his window.

She jogged to his car. "You can pull in there." She waved a hand, princess style, toward his garage.

"Is that so?"

She nodded and eyed him from beneath the bill of the cap. "Yep."

"Does this mean you're giving me permission, or you actually had the courage to tackle the mess?"

Her smile did funny things to his chest. "Both."

He couldn't hold his smile at bay. "You're taking over, huh?"

Her smile dissipated.

He leaned his head out of the vehicle. "Sarah, I'm kidding. I meant that in a good way."

She dropped her gaze and cleared her throat. "Proceed."

He hit the automatic unlock. The garage door chinked up to reveal an uncluttered, spacious garage.

"Amazing."

She walked beside his car. "There's actually a lot of room in here once it's organized."

"I meant that you're amazing, Sarah." He let his gaze linger as he exited the car. "I get the feeling you're buttering me up."

Her smile faded. Couldn't be a good sign. Something was up. Something bad.

Sarah climbed up a stepladder. "I put Donna's stuff up there. I didn't figure you'd want to get rid of it. So I boxed it carefully."

"I see." He studied her for a moment before re-scanning the garage. Then he looked back at her. "What's up?"

"We need to talk about something pretty important. It could affect whether you still want me here."

He leaned on the car. "We've needed to talk."

"Mina took the boys to the park and dinner for a few hours so we can." Her voice and hands trembled.

A deep wariness entered his bones as he waved her inside. "Go ahead."

"We should eat first." She set a platter of pot roast and potatoes on the table.

"Mina cook this?"

She blushed. "No. I did."

He smiled. "Then I can't wait to try it."

She laughed. "Don't get your hopes up."

After polishing off his second helping, Aaron pushed his plate away. "Okay, Donna, the suspense is killing me."

"Excuse me?" She paled.

"The suspense is killing me. Just spit it out."

She set her fork down. And scowled.

"Did I say something wrong?"

She shrugged and poked her peas. A little too hard. Stabbed would be a better word for it. "You called me 'Donna,'" she whispered. Then for whatever reason, tears began pouring from her eyes.

Before Aaron knew why, he rose and came around to her side of the table. She scooted her chair back to stand but he put his hands on her shoulders, preventing her escape.

Her face reddened. "I—I just need a few moments to compose myself."

"I understand. But I should apologize." He dropped his hands and raked fingers through his hair. "I really have no idea why that happened. I mean, you're nothing like her. And I mean that in a good way. In fact. I wish—" He sighed. "I shouldn't wish this but I wish she'd been more like you in some ways." He replaced his hands on her shoulders and stepped toward her.

Sarah shook her head and brushed his hands off. "No. No, Aaron. You don't." Her throat convulsed and she put her hands to her mouth as if to smother a sob.

"Sarah? What is it?" He wanted to hold her. It took every ounce of strength not to.

"Sit down, Aaron."

"I can't. Not until I know what's wrong. I need to know why my mistake upset you so." He swallowed hard.

"It's not your mistake that upset me. It's mine."

"Just tell me. Whatever it is, we'll work through it."

"Not this. Aaron, I could have been the one to kill your wife. I could have been the one responsible for leaving the children you love without their mother."

Aaron let the words sink in, but no matter how much he tried to make sense of them, he couldn't.

"I don't understand."

"Of course you wouldn't. Because I'm not who you think. I have a history of DUI. I was on my way to being a full-fledged alcoholic. In—in my past, I hit someone while driving drunk. A—a little child—"

But he'd already jerked and scrambled back as if she'd dealt physical blows.

He put his hands on the back of the chair and leaned forward. Was he about to throw up? He certainly looked like it. Like her words had caused him to buckle over with physical pain. Forehead in his hands, he slowly sat.

"Aaron, I'm sorry. When I signed up, I had no idea about Donna."

He shook his head and stood, but his steps were staggering as though drunk with grief. "I can't believe this about you, Sarah. I just can't."

"I'm sorry. As much as I wish it not to be true, it is."

"Saturday nights…"

"I go to AA. Not because I'm still struggling. But because I'm trying to help others to cope and be free."

Something hit him. Hard.

He met her gaze. "This is the reason you don't feel you can have a family of your own."

"Yes."

Then she needed a chance to heal.

And a chance to choose from a place of wholeness rather than brokenness.

Which meant he needed to release her from her contract.

And from his heart.

"Aaron, please say something."

Though she'd be devastated and assume he was sending her away for good, she needed a sabbatical. Cruel as it sounded, she wouldn't venture out any other way.

He met her gaze and said coolly, "I'll help you pack your things. You can stay in the cottage until a room is available at the bed-and-breakfast."

Chapter Eighteen

A pot holder hit him in the forehead. "Aaron Michael, I never dreamed in a million years that you'd send that poor girl away."

He clenched his jaw and swerved toward the kitchen island. "Not now, Mina."

"Oh, you don't wanna talk about it now? Well, when, then? Aaron Michael Petrowski, if you weren't so hulking big I'd turn you over my knee and swat your bottom until you came to your senses."

Sitting, he put his face in his hands. "I'm drained. I said I don't want to talk about it. But since you insist, I didn't send her away. I'm giving her the chance to choose with a clear conscience."

"Choose what?"

"Me. Us." His voice sounded as raw as it felt. "Suggesting she leave was one of the hardest things I've ever had to do."

"I think you're acting like a stubborn mule."

"No. I'm giving her a chance to choose outside her self-appointed vow."

"What do you mean?"

The door opened. "He here?" Ash walked in.

Last person he wanted to talk to.

Ash barreled across the room. "What the—"

Aaron punched the TV volume up.

"—is wrong with you, Aaron?"

"I'm in no mood for your mouth, Ash."

She removed her glasses. "So what are you in the mood for? A fight?" She moved to stand between him and his show.

"Yes. Especially if you don't remove yourself from in front of the TV."

"What's going on, Aaron? You've been a bear."

"You got your way, Ash." Mina swept through the room. "I'm going to bathe the boys."

"What do you mean? Where's Sarah? I thought she did that."

"*Did* being the key word." Mina stalked off.

"What happened? Did she leave?"

"I asked her to."

She sat. "So you know."

"Yes, and I also know how you bullied her about it." He clenched his teeth. "You had *no* right. She has tortured herself enough."

"I know. But I figured that out too late. So obviously, you love her?"

"Obviously, you don't know how to mind your own business. Now get out from the path of my TV."

"Why don't you go get her back?"

"Because she needs the freedom to be able to choose without being bound to a vow made out of fear of retribution."

"No idea what that means."

"You would if you'd get back to church."

"Fine. I'll drop it. But answer one question. Do you love her like you loved my best friend?"

"Leave Donna out of this."

"I really want to know."

"I care deeply about her."

"Why can't you just say you love her? There's nothing wrong with admitting it."

"I don't know."

"You don't know if you love her, or you don't know if you can admit it?"

"Both. Now move or get moved."

"Fine. Where is she?"

"I'm not telling you that."

"I'll find out on my own, then." She started off.

He kicked the recliner down and pursued. "Ash, where are you going?"

"To right my wrong and get her back, because I've never seen you in such a sour pathetic mood."

He surged and grabbed her arm. "Stay out of this."

"Let go."

"Do not interfere."

"Do not make me break out my third-degree black belt."

"You do and I'll break out mine. And I won't hold back just because you're a female."

"Since I know you mean that, I'll leave now."

He trailed her to the door. "*Where* are you going?"

"To mind my own business. And yours." She smirked.

"Don't go over there. Mind your own business. And stay out of mine."

"I'm not. Besides, I don't know where 'there' is."

"Right. Miss find-anyone-anywhere-anytime. What's behind all this, Ash?" He wanted to be sure Ash wasn't going to be cruel or get a wild hair and be nice and try to influence Sarah to come back before she'd had a chance to choose another family, and not just as their nanny. "Why would you try to find her?"

Ash turned and eyed him peculiarly. "Which 'her'?"

The blood drained from his face and chest. "What do you mean? There's only one *her.*"

Ash shook her head and for the first time in a long time, looked contrite and vulnerable. "No. There are two. And, yes, I'm going to find them both."

"Ashleigh, tell me what's going on. Right now."

"When I have my facts straight, I will. Besides, you know how I hate people siphoning information out of me or telling me what to do. So don't tell me what to do, because you doing that makes me want to do it more."

"You have a serious problem with authority."

"I was born three minutes before you, little brother. So technically I'm the one in authority here." She smiled, then grew serious and hugged him for the first time in years. "I won't do anything that isn't right," she whispered in his ear.

When Ash started to pull away, Aaron held her. How many times had he longed to comfort her when their parents had died? Yet she was so tough and self-sufficient, she hadn't afforded him the opportunity. So he relished the sibling affection now.

He reluctantly let her go. "Why do I get the feeling you intend to go mind Sarah's business, too? And, who is this second 'she'?"

She smirked. "Bye, Aaron. Enjoy your show."

"Ash…Ashleigh Kate! Come back here."

But, as usual, she ignored him as her long legs took her to her Hummer.

"What was that all about?" Mina came in with two soppy boys and had them stand by the warmth of the glowing gas log.

"Trust me, you don't want to know." Aaron hit the remote to turn it on.

"Where'd Ash go in such a rush?"

"Trust me. *I* don't want to know."

A late-night knock brought Sarah off her bed. She eyed her clock on the way to the door. Who would come after dark? Fear streaked through her. She eyed her lock. Good. Double bolted.

Aaron had been right: this place was creepy. He'd tried to protest when she refused to stay in the pool cottage.

Lack of vacancy elsewhere forced her to return to

the "ote." She rubbed her arms to abate the sudden chill in the room and walked toward the door with her cell phone poised to dial 9-1-1. She pressed the numbers but not the send button.

She peeked through the keyhole. A woman stood shivering in the snow. Sarah opened the door.

Then nearly closed it.

Ashleigh Petrowski stood on the other side. Sarah rolled her eyes. "You're the only person I know who'd wear movie-star big sunglasses in the middle of a winter night."

"And you're the only person I know besides my brother, my skip-tracing partner and Mina who has the guts to stand up to me enough to say something like that. Can I come in?"

No. I'd rather see you stand out in the freezing snow. Sarah licked her lips and lifted her chin. "That depends. Why are you here?"

"My brother is miserable. And I'm cold." She pushed her way in, forcing Sarah either to move it or lose it. So rather than get steamrolled, she got out of Ashleigh's way.

Ash removed her glasses and scarf and set her stylish clutch on the counter. She turned to face Sarah and leaned against the TV stand. For the first time, Sarah realized Ashleigh's eyes were red.

"Have you been crying?"

A grating sound came out of Ash. "Uh, no. Puhleez. It seems I've acquired an allergy." She averted her gaze and looked pained.

"To?"

Ash tilted her hip out and sent Sarah a don't-you-dare-say-I-told-you-so look. "The guineas."

Laughter sprayed through Sarah's lips though she tried to press them closed.

Ash rolled her eyes but looked close to laughing herself. "Sit. We need to chat."

"No, really, we need to duke it out. But you'd slaughter me. And there's no referee here to spare my life."

Now Ashleigh laughed. Then grew serious. "I'm here to apologize."

"You look as though the admission might kill you."

"Possibly. But I'm also here to make amends. I was wrong about you. And it was wrong the way I went about things."

"How do you know you were wrong about me?" Because Sarah needed to know as much as anyone that she wasn't who Ashleigh thought she was.

"I know because my brother loves you. He's miserable without you and miserable to be around. And if he loves you, then there must be something I missed. So I looked further."

"About?"

"You. And the situation."

"How?"

"Took another trip to Kentucky. Talked to more people. People who'd gone to church with you. Viewed public court documents. Among other things. But before I say what, I need to know how you feel about Aaron."

"I love him. And I love his boys."

"Well, it seems they love you, too. So I did some more digging. And I discovered some things that you might be interested in knowing."

"Such as?"

"Such as that my brother doesn't want to have to live without you. He sent you away because he was afraid you are so much a woman of your word that you'd feel bound by your words to stay. Then regret it later."

"I'd never—"

"I know. But he needs to know that you would choose him if given the choice to choose anyone else in the world. Mina talked to us about what Macy's mom said to you in court. He wanted to give you time to heal from this self-vow and fear of never having children. Because he's convinced that could skew your feelings toward him."

"I know God brought me here. I also know God has forgiven me. And I know that I probably have a skewed view of why I didn't want to be a mother. But once I grew attached to your family and sensed this was the one God wanted me to have, that fear lifted. Gone. As if maybe I've believed the lie all these years. I understand I'm completely forgiven and free."

"Free to the point you'd still choose Aaron if given the choice to meet someone else and make your own family?"

"Yes. I have dated in the past. And cared deeply for men. But nothing like what I feel for Aaron. I love him, with everything in me. I want to make a life with him, and the boys."

"But not just for the boys—because you've grown attached to them?"

"No. Aaron will still be there long after the boys are grown and out of the house. And I want to be there with Aaron."

"You know this for sure?"

"Yes."

"Do you also know that the girl you hit did survive?"

Her throat closed. "I knew she did at first. But I wrote and never heard from her. Or her parents. I'd hoped—"

"She is."

"Still alive?"

"Yes."

Sarah faced Ash. "What do you know?"

"Sit down, Sarah."

Her heart pounded. "You looked."

"Yes. And found her. She has been getting your letters. But her parents wanted her to wait until she was seventeen to contact you. Her birthday is next month. She wants to meet you."

"I don't know if I can do this. Is she mad?"

"Not at all."

"I don't understand."

"I do, but I can't tell you. I promised her I wouldn't. You'll know when you meet her."

"How can she not be angry? How did she and her parents ever learn to forgive me?"

"I'll let Macy tell you that."

"Is there something I need to know that you're not telling me?"

Ash's silence didn't make Sarah feel good.

"I'm telling you everything I can. Answers will come when you meet her."

"Since the accident I've dreamed of nothing but meeting her. But now I'm not sure I can."

Surprisingly, Ash sat next to Sarah and covered her tightly clenched hands with her own. "Trust me on this, Sarah. You need to go."

"Trust you?" Aaron snorted and started to step away from his whacked-out sister, who claimed she'd found and conducted an amicable visit with Sarah the previous night.

She bolted forward and grabbed his arm. "Aaron, wait. I've never asked you for anything so important to me."

Important? Regarding Sarah?

He leaned in and felt Ash's forehead.

She jerked her head backward and knocked his hand away, giving a long-suffering, concessive sigh. "Look. I know I was wrong. And I'm not out to scheme or scam or otherwise ruin Sarah. I'm not *that* ruthless. Especially since I know how much you care about one another."

He narrowed his gaze. "How would you know that?"

"Because she's not afraid to say what she wants. And she wants to be with you, Aaron. And not just as the nanny."

"And what about the boys?"

"I think you know the answer to that. She loves them as if they were her own."

He nodded, believing, knowing that. An enormous sense of gratitude overwhelmed him. Ready to listen now, he sat across from Ash. "Fine. I'm all ears. Talk."

"Aaron, you need to go with Sarah to meet her."

"Why?"

"Trust me. You just do."

"Do you know things you didn't tell her?"

"Yes. Things that will make it very hard for Sarah when they meet. Sarah knows I couldn't share everything. But I promised Macy, that's the girl's name, that I wouldn't say anything to Sarah because she's afraid if Sarah knew, she'd feel too bad to come."

"Can you give me a clue?"

"Well, I didn't exactly promise Macy I wouldn't tell you. I just gave her my word Sarah wouldn't find out until minutes before the meeting. By the way, Macy is who Sarah's been writing to."

He nodded and sat. "Spill."

"She's in a wheelchair."

Aaron stood. "From the accident?"

"Yes. It shattered her legs from the knees down. Damaged the nerves."

He sat. "Were they amputated?"

"No, but her legs don't work."

He rose. "There are robotic prostheses."

"Her parents have checked, but they are expensive

and experimental and therefore insurance won't cover it. Macy's parents opted not to sue Sarah's family."

Aaron sat.

"Keep still. You look like a yo-yo."

"I might have a way around the cost." He thought of the program for wounded vets. "I'll make some phone calls. That way I don't offer something I can't produce. Sarah knows you found her?"

"Yes. She knows everything except the extent of the injuries."

"She'll be devastated."

"But she'll also be free."

"Are you free?"

"Yes." Sarah's heart warmed to the welcoming sound of Aaron's voice after not hearing it for weeks. How she'd missed him and the boys. And had prayed for this moment.

Thank You.

She leaned into the phone. "When?"

"This afternoon. I'd like to talk over coffee."

"I'd like that, too." Though she desperately wanted to see the boys, she first needed to talk one-on-one with Aaron.

And convince the stubborn brute that, given any other choice in the world, she'd still choose him.

"I'll pick you up at two."

"I'll be ready."

Two o'clock took forever to arrive. Sarah checked her hair and makeup in the mirror for the gazillionth obsessive time. No way was she wearing the hideous steel-wool sweater. Okay, so it wasn't really steel, but might as well be.

An image of Christmas Day and of Aaron opening the putrid sweater flashed into her mind. She snickered and faced her closet. "The tradition of passing the sweater should live on. And Aaron will be the innocent victim—err—lucky recipient this year." Yes. That was what she'd do.

If today went as she hoped.

Footsteps outside caused her to whirl. She went and opened the door.

"Hey, Sarah." Aaron stood as leisurely as a rigid military guy could.

She stepped out onto the porch. "Hi." Suddenly she felt shy. Until he extended his hand, palm up. She eyed it and put her hand in his. His lopsided grin said it all.

Relief caused tears to prick her eyes.

He wasn't here to say goodbye.

After driving her to Square Beans, a coffee shop on the Refuge town square, which was actually a circle, they chatted about the boys.

"So Ash tells me she stopped by." Aaron cradled his cup between his hands.

"Yes. She was quite nice, actually."

Aaron nodded. "She mentioned she'd found Macy."

Sarah swallowed her coffee. "Yes. Macy wants to meet me."

Aaron reached for her hand. "I'd like to go with you."

She squeezed back. "I'd like that, too."

"Any idea when this will go down?"

"Macy's parents actually called me. They—" She cleared her throat of the sudden emotional clog. "They've arranged to meet me next Saturday. I agreed. I know that you go to Joel's on Satur—"

"I'd rather go with you. Mina has already agreed to watch the boys. And, miracle of all miracles, Ash offered her babysitting services, too."

Sarah laughed. "Something tells me they'll be loaded up on sugar."

Aaron chuckled and brushed a thumb along her hand. "Ash does like to try to spoil them. Sugar. Noisy toys. Toys that have a million tiny pieces. Yeah, that's Ash."

"Not to mention toys that like to hide in my rug's carpet fibers and poke the bottoms of my feet at night. I—I mean the rug in my old room."

"Sarah, we miss you. The boys miss you. I want you to come back."

Her heart rate sped, then dipped. "As the nanny?"

Several seconds ticked by before he would answer. He eyed her as if calculating a parachute drop from the air.

Finally, he squeezed her hand and said, "We'll talk about that after we meet Macy on Saturday. Okay?"

"Okay."

Why wouldn't he talk about her status, their status, now? Was that good news or bad?

He stood, reaching for their coats. The way he

draped hers over her, then let his hands linger on her shoulders hopefully meant the news would be good.

She would know after Saturday.

Right now, meeting Macy took precedence. Between the upcoming meeting with Macy and her parents, and the ensuing "where are we and where do we go from here" talk on the horizon with Aaron, the next few days and weeks would prove life-altering.

But would Saturday and the days to follow change her world for better? Or for worse?

"What time are you supposed to meet Macy?"

"Noon. I offered to drive to Paducah, but they said they'd rather come to Refuge and meet me. They heard about the bridge collapse in the news and wanted to come here and see the town that claimed, even in calamity, to live up to its name."

Back at the "ote" Aaron walked her to her door. "I'm not real keen on you staying here."

"I'll keep my doors locked."

"You won't stay here long." He dipped his head and planted a chaste kiss on her cheek. But when his gaze dragged down her cheek and across her mouth, she knew this was not the kind of kiss he desired.

"I'll pick you up at eleven. See you Saturday."

Saturday. The day she'd dreamed of since that fateful night had changed her life had arrived. Now she'd enter a new kind of normal.

She didn't want to spend the rest of her life after

today and after her conversation with Aaron wishing for her life to go back to the way it used to be.

She'd spent so many years after her bout with alcoholism and the accident doing that. And had finally grown to accept that her lot in life would mean she'd never get to be a mother.

Lord, You will always be my heart's desire. People tend to either think too highly of themselves, or too little. You know that I fall under the latter most of the time. But I'm choosing this day to trust that, despite my screwups, You do have a future worth hoping for in store for me.

Aaron's SUV pulled into the lot.

Sarah held tightly to her chest the Bible she hadn't realized she'd lifted and opened, melding its promises to her heart. "My future is in Your hands. I'll be okay."

"You okay?" Aaron asked Sarah after she got into the car.

"Nervous, but yes."

Aaron could not believe the calm in Sarah's demeanor. "It doesn't show. That you're nervous, I mean."

"Trust me, when we get to the Cone Zone, my heart will try to claw out through my throat."

He laughed and turned down the road. Immediately he caught vision of the vehicle Macy's father had described—a forest-green family van.

Only one green Kentucky-licensed vehicle sat in the parking lot. He eyed his watch. Right on time. Had to be it.

"I expected a minivan." Sarah's voice quivered as she eyed the vehicle.

The van was larger, and had an obvious opening for a wheelchair lift.

Tears sprang to Sarah's eyes.

He grasped her hand. "Sarah, before we go in, Macy asked me to share something with you."

Sarah trembled all over. "You spoke with her?"

"Yes, when her father called me for directions and asked the best place to meet. I've arranged with the owners to have the back room reserved. You and Macy's family will have privacy."

"And you?"

"I won't leave your side."

"Aaron, what—what's the wheelchair lift about? Is that for one of Macy's parents?"

He squeezed her hand, wishing what he was about to say hadn't come about. "No. Macy is in a wheelchair. She asked me to wait to tell you until you got here."

"Why?"

"Why did she ask me to wait to tell you?"

Tears streaked down Sarah's face and her throat convulsed. Her face grew red. "No, why is she in a wheelchair? When? From the accident?"

"Yes."

Sarah's composure crumpled. Face in hands, she bent forward, trying to hold her shirt against her mouth. But in a great heave, her shoulders gave a massive quake. A subdued wail came from deep in her gut.

Aaron clicked off his seat belt and leaned over her, resting his hands on her back, which had grown hot and damp with sweat. "I know. I know this is hard. Go ahead and cry. Get it out."

Though her sobs quieted, her shoulders still trembled violently. He unhooked her seat belt and pulled her against his chest. The entire time she wept, Aaron prayed. For her. For Macy. For them and what the future starting now would hold.

What had to be ten minutes later, his cell phone rang. He eyed the number. Just as he thought. Macy's father.

"Hello. Yes. We're here but we'll be just a few more minutes. If you all want to go ahead and order, that would be good. Ah, pepperoni for me and sausage for Sarah. Thanks."

Aaron hung up and held Sarah. A couple seconds later she lifted her head. "Was that Macy?"

"Her dad."

Sarah dug around her purse for a package of tissues and antibacterial cloths. She tugged one out, wiped her blotchy face, and blew her nose.

She stared silently at the building for five solid minutes before turning to Aaron. "I'm ready. Let's go."

Chapter Nineteen

Melted rubber. That's what Sarah's legs felt like as she wobbled across the floor of the family-owned establishment known as the Cone Zone, which boasted the best homemade ice cream and pizza this side of the Mississippi. Even cantaloupe ice cream—her favorite.

She'd be tasting none of that today. For if any sort of substance entered her mouth in the near future, she'd surely see it again.

The hostess met them, briefly stalling to eye Sarah's face. She knew her eyes were probably still puffy and her skin blotchy. But there was simply no help for it.

She needed to g   nd face the music, setting pride aside.

She had nothing to lose at this point. Macy had had everything to lose. And, apparently, unfortunately, thanks to Sarah, had lost *a lot*. The use of her legs, at least. Aaron had filled her in on the details on the way in.

Aaron held her steady as they entered the private room. When Sarah's gaze found the very beautiful young woman, rather than the child she remembered, in the wheelchair, tears threatened to gush again. Until Macy's mother rushed her. "Sarah, we know this is a shock."

How on earth could the mother find it in her heart to comfort the very person who had sentenced her daughter to life in that chair?

The urge to run out of here and harm herself came over Sarah. She should have been the one hurt. Not Macy. Not Macy.

Macy gave a feeble smile as her father, more subdued than the mother, wheeled her over to Sarah.

Aaron stood by, stalwart and strong. Where she trembled his hand supported. He looked close to choking up a couple of times. And she felt the compassion of God through the ends of his fingers. Glimpsed the mercy of God through Macy's eyes.

But how could this be? Especially after what they'd each lost at the hands of her wrong choices and the other driver like her?

Those thoughts tried to rule until the strongest sense of God's presence and forgiveness that she'd ever known came upon her.

She sensed His power surging through this meeting and the miracle it meant for them all. God through Aaron was her source of strength in these enormously difficult, yet no less than glorious, moments.

Macy was alive. And that's what mattered. Right?

Macy's father and a younger man helped her to stand. Macy's legs wobbled, too. But Sarah knew that was probably from her injuries and weak muscles from unworkable legs rather than nervousness.

Sarah moved forward. And the moment the women embraced, Sarah broke again.

Macy swallowed against her shoulder. "I'm glad to finally meet you."

What? Glad? *What?*

Sarah held her tighter. "I'm sorry. I'm so sorry. If I could take it back—"

"I might not have wanted you to." Macy leaned back, tears in her eyes. Then, to Sarah's utter confounding, she smiled. "Sit?"

Gladly. Her legs were about to give out.

At the thought of Macy's legs, Sarah started crying again. But Macy should not be the one to comfort her. Sarah held back her emotion. "I don't understand how you can be so gracious to me." She held Macy's kind but emotional gaze. Then her mother's and father's. They nodded at her, but said nothing.

"Obviously, this is difficult for all of us. I do appreciate you meeting me. And letting me tell you how sorry I am in person." Sarah swallowed hard. "I—I can't take back what I did, or—or change this." Her hand swept the arms of the wheelchair. "But I wish with everything in me that I could. I'm so very sorry. I don't know what else to say."

In the ensuing silence, Sarah felt like fleeing.

Until she felt a set of hands come to rest on her shoulders. She looked up. Aaron. Of course.

She felt pressure of his hands resting on her shoulder, infusing her with the strength to stay and stick this meeting out, and to speak from her heart her sorrow and regret, no matter how humbling or hard.

Macy's family needed that.

What mattered was that she'd stripped a child of her ability to walk, and nearly stripped a set of loving parents of their child.

Macy's mother approached Sarah. "There are things you don't know. Details about that night that you should hear."

Sarah nodded.

"That night we left Macy with a young babysitter to attend a party down the street. It was drizzly, so we drove instead of walked. We thought Macy was sleeping, but she woke up to a dark house. She got scared and went to look for us. Which is why she was crossing the street. The babysitter got distracted by a phone call, or fell asleep, we're not sure. She didn't hear Macy wake up or see her slip out. Our car was at the neighbors' and she saw lights and heard laughter. So she came to find us." Macy's mom drew a shuddering breath.

Macy's father took her hand and cleared his throat. "Macy never saw you coming."

"And I didn't see her until too late."

"Even had you not been drinking, you probably would have hit her," Macy's dad continued.

"I don't believe that. I'll never believe that and I will never take another drink in my life."

"We know that."

Aaron put his hand on her back. He was handling this quite well for a man who'd lost his wife the same way this child had lost her ability to walk.

Sarah reached for Macy. "I'm so sorry that I took away your ability to walk."

"But I *am* walking. Don't you see? I am walking with Him. All my life I've known someone's been praying for me. When Mom and Dad started giving me your letters, I figured out that all along that person was you."

"I don't understand."

"We weren't believers," Macy's mom explained.

"There weren't really any Christians to speak of in our family," Macy's dad added.

Macy gripped Sarah's hand. "I've felt a connection with you through your letters and I forgave you a long time ago. I came to know God through your letters and, eventually, so did my parents."

"But—"

"Your bad judgment was just that, bad judgment. You learned the hard way."

"I learned at the expense of you, your legs and your ability to walk. You can't walk because I drove drunk."

"But I walk with the Lord because you wrote the letters."

Sarah started to shake her head. To protest. But Macy's imploring eyes stopped her. "Your letters helped me find God."

Sarah smiled as much as she could. "I still pictured you as little. I don't know why I was so surprised to walk in and find that you'd grown up. I guess I feared you hadn't. My mind remembered you as you were the night I saw you. Small. Scared. Hurt. Alone."

Macy smiled. "But I wasn't alone. Some people would have driven off. But you stayed with me."

"You remember?"

"Yes. I'll never forget your face. You were more afraid than I was. Your face and your tears are all I remember. That and you holding my hand and covering me from the rain until the ambulance came. I still have the coat you covered me up with."

"I still have your backpack. I carry it almost everywhere."

Macy's dad looked at her. "We didn't want it because it reminded us of our negligence in getting a too-young sitter without vetting her level of responsibility."

"She's messed up. I've tried writing her. But—"

Macy's mom took her hand. "She never felt responsible. Has never owned up. So, you see, Sarah. It was all of our faults."

Sarah nodded, choosing to accept that. She smiled at Macy. "So does this mean we keep in touch?"

Macy grinned full-on. "I'd love that."

"Me, too. I feel I've made a friend today."

"No, you've *met* a friend today. I've known you for years, Sarah. Now it's time for you to get to know me. In hard times, your letters were a lifeline. The poems and scriptures you sent always spoke to whatever was going on in my life."

Sarah faced Macy's parents. "Then thank you for allowing me to write her."

Sarah's mom teared up. "Sarah, one more thing. I'm told you don't feel worthy to be a mother. Quite possibly because of what I said to you in court. How I cursed you and said that your children would pay for your actions. It seems I wrecked your life, too."

"Nothing like what I've done to yours. You had every right to be angry and lash out."

She took Sarah's hand. "But I never dreamed my words would have lifelong impact on you."

Sarah sandwiched her hands over Macy's mom's. "And I never dreamed a few drinks could hurt so many lives for so very long."

Macy's mom nodded. "Yes, it would have been better had you never taken a drink. Yes, it would have been better had we made better choices that night, too." She eyed Aaron. "Because we all know that not every story has this kind of outcome."

The looks passing between Macy's parents and Aaron meant they knew about Donna. Sarah peered at Aaron in trepidation.

Aaron nodded and squeezed her shoulder. "But thankfully God has redeemed this situation."

Chapter Twenty

Aaron approached Sarah where she stood at the counter, having come over to help Mina.

"There's a shindig going on at the DZ tonight. Would you do me the honor of accompanying me?"

She continued to chop celery for salad. "Sure. What kind of shindig?"

"Joel and Amber sent video from Asia of the orphans they're adopting. We're all watching it on the big screen in the lobby of the DZ," he fibbed his head off.

"Sure. What time do you need the boys ready?"

"Mina will take care of that. In the meantime, why don't you take a day off and go to the mall. Buy yourself a pretty dress to wear this evening."

She squished her eyebrows together. "How fancy is this shindig?"

"It's a celebration. So dress accordingly."

"Semi-formal? Or church clothes?"

"Somewhere in between, since our church is jeans-on-Sunday casual. I'll pick you up back here around four-thirty. Dinner's at the DZ at five sharp."

She shot him a sassy salute and grinned. "Sir, yes, sir."

He shook his head and stepped out.

Mina entered looking guilty. "What?"

"What?" Sarah straightened.

"I asked you first."

"No, I asked you first. I think."

Mina averted eye contact. "Nothing. I'm just distracted today." Mina scrubbed the same spot on the counter for three full minutes. "Sooo, Aaron mention the film tonight?"

"He did."

"You should buy a nice dress."

"What—"

"Nope. That's all I'm gonna say. Buy a nice dress and get your hair done. Your roots are showing. And put some makeup on, too."

"I always wear makeup."

"I mean, some really snazzy makeup."

"I didn't get the idea this thing was that fancy."

Mina looked at her pointedly. "Becoming a mother is a very, very big deal."

"You're right. Amber and Joel deserve to have us celebrate, even though they won't be here to celebrate with us. When do they return from overseas?"

"Soon. Then they go back in a few months again. And that time, they may get to bring at least one of the children home."

* * *

"I've never felt so frivolous," Sarah said hours later as Mina helped her on with the necklace that went with the dress she'd purchased at the mall earlier.

"Shh. And hold still. He'll be here to pick us up any moment. And you came home late from shopping."

Sarah laughed at Mina's fussing. "The man gave me a credit card, a day off and ordered me to the mall. What do you expect?"

Mina laughed. "Point taken. Now hold still."

"Miss Sarah, you look pretty." Bryce's eyes grew luminous as he came close to peer at her.

"Yeah. Daddy's gonna be so happy you dressed up." Braden giggled. Bryce rushed him, and clamped a hand over his mouth, then eyed Sarah with big eyes.

Everyone was acting strangely today. Something was in the air. Season change. Cold weather. Something.

"Hello?" Aaron's voice trailed through the house.

Sarah whirled. He stopped at the door. Was he in an... "Air Force Dress uniform?"

Aaron stepped closer, taking her in from head to toe. His sturdy, open assessment caused her cheeks to heat. "You look great, Sarah."

She could only nod as he took her elbow with one arm and Bryce's hand with the other. "Everyone ready?"

Mina took Braden's hand and nodded to Aaron, then to the box in her hands. "Ready."

"Ready?" Aaron whispered into his phone moments later as Sarah was distracted buckling in Bryce. "Because we're on our way."

"Yep. We're waiting on you guys," Joel assured him. He and Amber had actually flown back two days ago, and helped Aaron prepare for this evening. And his undercover proposal. The adoption film was a cover for the real operation at hand.

Aaron eyed Sarah and smiled. If she suspected, she didn't let on.

He eyed Mina and the box, which held three rings. Two small pinky rings set with two Air Force-blue stones to represent his sons. The stones also captured the beauty and shade of her eyes.

The other ring was a bit fancier and boasted a diamond that had taken an enormous bite out of his savings. Yet it would look delicious on her finger because of the hope and future it symbolized.

As they pulled up to the DZ, Aaron watched Sarah eye the parking lot. "Wow. Lots of people here. Seems like half the town showed up."

He grinned. Little did she know half the people inside weren't from Refuge, but were her friends and family from Kentucky. Even Macy and her parents had heard of Aaron's plans and asked to come. Sarah and Macy's friendship had bloomed beyond imagination.

Aaron held the door while Mina led the boys in. Two steps inside the door, Aaron steered Sarah toward the dimly lit room's edge.

"Wow. They went all out. I wish they'd called me to help decorate. This had to take some work," Sarah said, eyeing the formally draped tables and candles that provided the only light. After all, he didn't want her to see her friends and folks, waiting off to the sides and back out of view.

Once Sarah and Aaron were seated near the table in the front with Mina and the boys, Aaron motioned to Vince, who motioned for Sarah's friends and family to trickle in and seat themselves at tables in the back, behind Sarah so it would take her longer to notice them.

Brockton Drake stepped up to the microphone. "Ladies and gentlemen, thanks for coming. And now, without further ado, we'll begin." Brock's grin grew gargantuan as he stepped from the stage and passed by their table.

Aaron should trip him for winking at Sarah. Aaron eyed her. She didn't seem to suspect. Good.

The movie started. Sarah smiled as celebratory worship music that Ben had composed came on. Images scrolled across the screen in a PowerPoint-type presentation. Captions at the bottom of each photo of Joel and Amber and the children they were adopting rolled in a slide show. Suddenly those pictures faded and the music changed.

The moment had drawn near. Aaron turned his body to face Sarah. But her eyes blinked in confusion at the screen, which went white for a few moments before images of her, Bryce and Braden, Mina and Aaron started scrolling across instead.

Confusion on her face mounted as the music grew softer and more romantic.

Then a final picture of Aaron and the boys dressed

identically and holding out three pink roses, her favorite color, became the focal point. The pictures stopped scrolling on that image.

Then slowly, the words he'd carefully planned began to scroll across the screen. "Sarah, we love you. Will you marry us?"

Sarah blinked at the picture of Aaron, Bryce and Braden, then at the words. She tilted her head slowly to peer at Aaron. "Wha—?"

Aaron knelt in front of her. Tears sprang to her eyes. "Sarah, will you do me the honor of becoming my wife? You'll make a wonderful mother to my boys and beyond. Will you stop being our nanny, and be our bride and stepmom instead?"

"Is this for real?" she breathed.

Aaron nodded.

Sarah's hand came to her mouth. "Oh, I wish my mom could be—"

"Right here, baby."

Sarah turned to face her mom, who wept with an open grin. Sarah started recognizing people in the room, and realizing what this truly was.

"I've been gloriously duped and set up." She giggled. And couldn't stop.

Everyone laughed.

Bryce, Braden and Aaron stood side by side and extended hands that held open felt-lined boxes with rings sparkling in the flickering candlelight.

"Oh!" Taking in the rings, Sarah dashed forward and hugged Aaron with arms that could rival a boa constrictor. "Yes, Aaron. Oh, yes! You have just made me the happiest woman on earth." She leaned back and pulled Bryce and Braden, both giggling, into a four-person hug.

After celebratory hugs, catcalls, endless clapping and congratulations, Aaron and Sarah took the boys to the refreshment table, which a local coffee shop owner had catered.

"Pudding!" Braden jumped up and down and up and down.

"Chocolate!" Bryce sent Aaron a pleading look.

"Since it's a special occasion, I'll let you have sugar just this once."

"Yay!"

Bryce, pudding precariously in hand, scrambled up into Sarah's lap. "You like your ring from me?"

"More than you'll ever know." She recognized the rings were mother's rings. Her voice grew tight at Aaron's thoughtfulness, and God's, in that He'd granted her a desire so deep in her heart. She hadn't realized how much it meant until this moment of its fulfillment.

That the boys and Aaron would be in her life in this capacity forever was just out of this world and—

A cold splat. Pudding. She knew it before she even looked down.

"Whoops!" Bryce eyed her dress, right beneath her shoulder. "I'm sorry!"

She smiled and bent her forehead against his. "It's okay. We'll dab it with a napkin."

Aaron had already leaned over the table and retrieved a clean one.

"I hope you'll get used to seeing all manner of stains on the clothes you buy me, Aaron. Such is the way when you have children." She took the napkin and started to dab.

Aaron caught her hand in his. Grinned wide. "I'm a man who happens to think that motherhood is stunning." He leaned over and dipped his finger in the pudding without quite making contact with her. "And chocolate happens to be my favorite."

"Hey, I thought you didn't like sugar."

"That's because I've never tried it on you before." His grin became both bold and impish. And Sarah had to turn away before her cheeks combusted into flames.

Someone tinkled a spoon against a glass. Sarah and Aaron looked up to see who.

"Ash?" They looked at one another in disbelief. But only for a moment. Aaron pulled her as close as was proper. "That sound means we're supposed to kiss."

"Is that so?"

"Yes." And he certainly did. "I'm a strong man who can do a lot of hard things. But living without you isn't one of them. I've missed you. The boys missed you." He swallowed. "They cried every night you were gone."

She blinked back tears. "Me, too. I missed them," she whispered. "And you. And Mina." She laughed. "I don't know how, but I even missed those fuzzy rodents. And, believe it or not, I missed Ash, too."

More tinkling sounded.

Sarah smiled, leaned in and met his kiss.

After ear-thundering applause and another tender kiss, Aaron leaned his head back to peer at her, yet still held her close. "But what if someone younger comes along? A sweeter deal?"

"Then I'll introduce him to your sour sister. God knows she needs someone to love that meanness right out of her."

"So you know it's not just you she's hostile with, right?"

"Yes, but Ash had a point. Her instincts were on target. Don't be mad at her for looking out for you."

He leaned his head back even farther. His brows rose. "Are you sticking up for Ashleigh?"

"Yes. Just don't tell her."

He chuckled. "Under one condition."

"What's that?"

"You don't tell her I told you I caught her sneaking the address from those child sponsorship forms you left in your room."

"What? She really did?"

"She really did. I noticed she got a letter from her sponsored child the other day, too."

"I'm completely amazed. God's working in her heart."

"And He used you to do it."

"I wouldn't say that."

"Well, what would you say?"

"At the moment?" Her gaze dropped to his mouth.

"Yeah."

"I'd say hush up and kiss me again."

"Well, gentleman that I am, it'd be rude to deny a lady's request. Come here, you." He pulled her into his arms for a hug and a kiss on top of her head.

She groaned. "Not that kind of kiss. I was thinking more along these lines." She blinked her eyelashes against his cheek.

Aaron pulled her close and swayed to soft worship music. "I could go crazy kissing you, Sarah. Go crazy trying not to." Boldness and humor flashed in his eyes.

She leaned in. "Then stop trying so hard."

He shot her a salute and a grin. "Ma'am, yes, ma'am." Then the brute bent in and rubbed her nose with his.

"Daddy! We didn't know you knew how to butterfly kiss!"

"Eskimo!"

"Butterfly!"

"Boys!" Aaron pointed to the dessert table. "Go eat sugar."

Sarah giggled. "Did you just order them to go eat—?"

He pulled her close again. "Yes. But I had a clandestine motive."

She grinned as their lips finally met once more.

"I can't kiss you properly if you're laughing," he said a moment later.

"I'm not laughing. I'm happy."

"For?"

"All of us."

Gaze deepening, he pulled her close and sealed their love, and their future, with another kiss. A grown-up one that had nothing to do with butterflies or noses.

But one driven by fierce emotion over knowing God had brought them to this place.

Their embrace deepened with assurance that God had brought her here with every intention of her completing this skydiving soldier daddy's family.

* * * * *

Dear Reader

This story speaks of loss and hope. Loss touches each of us in this life. There's no escaping it. If you have not gone through something hard in your life, eventually you will. But likewise, hope does not disappoint. We have the God of all hope who loves us and is intimate with our pain. He also knows our dreams and hopes. I pray that hope touches your life and heart profoundly, even in the face of any loss or heartache you face. May you always seek Refuge in the haven of His wings. Your readership is a tremendous blessing. Thank you for spending time with me in Refuge, the fictional town that lives up to its name.

If you would like to sign up for my quarterly newsletter for a chance to receive great prizes and updates on new releases, visit my Web site at www.cherylwyatt.com and input your e-mail address in the newsletter sign-up space provided. I respect your privacy and will not share your information with a third party.

I love hearing from readers. I invite you to e-mail me at Cheryl@CherylWyatt.com or write me at P.O. Box 2955, Carbondale, IL 62902-2955.

Cheryl Wyatt

QUESTIONS FOR DISCUSSION

1. In this story, Sarah struggles with fear of being a mother because of mistakes she made in her past. Could you sympathize with her in this, and do you think this is why she pursued a career in child care? Why or why not?

2. Do you think that Macy and her family should have easily forgiven Sarah for her actions? Why or why not?

3. Do you think Aaron made the right choice in returning to work? If so, how so?

4. Why do you think Ashleigh is the way she is in this story? Were you endeared enough to her by the end of the book to want to see Ash have her own story? Why or why not? I would love e-mail feedback on this character.
cheryl@cherylwyatt.com

5. The twins lost their mom when they were eight weeks of age, so they long for a mother. Do you think this was believable/ plausible? And if so, why and how so?

6. Sarah brings light and laughter into Aaron's home. What do you think it was about her that accomplished this?

7. Do you think Aaron and Sarah should have tried harder to fight off their attraction to one another since she was his employee? Why or why not?

8. In this story, Officer Stallings recognized Sarah, but didn't reveal her secret even though he was friends with Aaron. Did you respect him for this? Why or why not?

9. Could you understand and relate to Sarah's difficulty in attending church? Why or why not?

10. Aaron's pararescue team wanted to be able to help the community recover from a bridge collapse. How do you think the three programs they proposed would benefit the town?

11. The scripture theme for this story is based on God's promise that hope does not disappoint. In what ways do you think that applied to the story and the characters?

12. What did you think about Bryce having an imaginary gaggle of geese? Do you think Aaron's response to this was best? Why or why not? And if not, how should he have handled it?

13. In what way did Braden and Bryce differ in this story? Did you find that unusual for twins? Which

one of them do you think will grow up to be most like Aaron? Why so?

14. Twin Braden liked to push the limits. Do you think he would have been as strong-willed had his mother not died? In what ways will this leadership trait benefit Braden in fulfilling his God-given destiny when he's older?

Love Inspired® SUSPENSE

RIVETING INSPIRATIONAL ROMANCE

Watch for our new series of
edge-of-your-seat suspense novels.
These contemporary tales
of intrigue and romance
feature Christian characters
facing challenges to their faith...
and their lives!

Steeple
Hill®

Visit:
www.SteepleHill.com